VESTA DIVIDED

STERLING R. WALKER

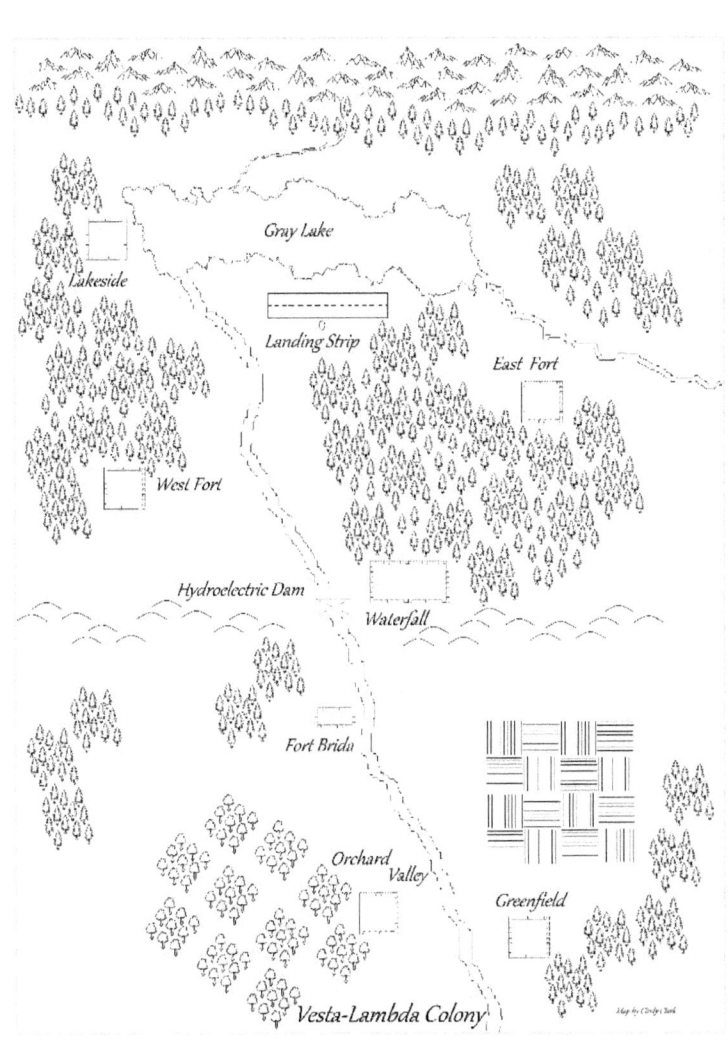

Gray Lake

Lakeside

Landing Strip

East Fort

West Fort

Hydroelectric Dam

Waterfall

Fort Brida

Orchard Valley

Greenfield

Vesta-Lambda Colony

Map by C Doğu's Book

ONE
FEVER

A sharp, stabbing pain in his right side wrenched Corban Abrams from an uneasy slumber. He bit his lip, trying not to make a sound and wake one of his roommates. He felt guilty sleeping on the only bed in Seventh Fort while the two women who kept vigil over him slept in blankets on the hardwood floor of his room.

The gunshot wound began to bother Corban shortly after everyone had retired for the night. The pain at the exit wound in his back spiked at random intervals, making restful sleep impossible. Although he'd been on the mend for several days, he knew he wouldn't be able to hide this new pain much longer. Plus, everyone was sure to notice his sweat-soaked sheets in the morning.

Let them sleep, for now. He attempted to reposition himself onto his left side without making the bedsprings squeak. His wound sent up another warning throb, but he squeezed his eyes shut and took measured breaths until the pain eased. Corban wiped his damp forehead on the edge of his sheet and tried to go back to sleep.

***

He was standing on the far side of the wide bridge, looking toward the landing strip, when it happened.

The explosion knocked him backward, off his feet. Corban watched in horror as a geyser of fire shot skyward. In moments, the landing strip was engulfed in clouds of smoke. He couldn't see any of the ships. He couldn't even see the bridge or the river, the smoke was so thick.

Coughing, he sat up, eyes watering as he tried to see through the haze, tried to make out which ship was on fire, but he couldn't tell. Fire raged over the entire tarmac, flames licking the sky. Whichever ship had exploded, it must have obliterated most of the others.

***

"*Nooooo!*" There were hands on his shoulders, shaking him.

"Corban! Corban, wake up!" Nikki Ramirez was standing over him. Even in the darkness he could tell it was her because he could hear her thoughts. *You had the premonition again, didn't you?*

Nikki's mother, Solona Zegarelli, stood on other side of his bed. He didn't have time to answer before Solona was berating him. "You're burning up! Why didn't you tell us? Quick, Nikki, fetch a bucket of water and get the lavender oil from my bag!"

"What's going on?" Corban's older brother, Thane, barged into the room, rubbing sleep from his eyes. "What happened?"

"I need a light." Solona didn't take time to explain. "Get some lamps, quickly."

"Here's one." Nikki lit their oil lamp and held it up for Solona.

"I'll get the one from my room." Thane left and was back in less than a minute, a glowing lamp in his hand.

With the light, Nikki and Thane were able to carry out Solona's orders. A flurry of activity produced Solona's medical bag and a bucket of cold water. Nikki was shooed out of the room before Solona and Thane gave Corban a vigorous sponge bath that left his teeth chattering.

"Is this really necessary?" Corban protested to an unsympathetic audience.

Solona peeled away the thick bandages covering both the entrance and exit wounds on his side. She grimaced when she uncovered the stitches on his back. "I should've caught this earlier. Thane, tell Rupert to send a message to Dr. DeKalb. Tell her I need thyme."

"You need . . . a clock?" Thane squinted at her.

"No, I need t-h-y-m-e. It's an herb. I'll need to make compresses for the infection."

"But shouldn't he have antibiotics?" Thane exchanged a worried glance with Corban when Solona said *infection*.

"There aren't any." Solona's lips were pinched into a paper-thin line. "The colony is out of medicine. Hopefully there's some on the new ship, but chances are it's expired, and we don't have time to wait for someone to open the airlock."

"Yes, ma'am. I'll tell Rupert." Thane limped to the door and closed it behind himself. He shared a room with his friend Rupert Conquist across the hall. Rupert's Talent for sending mental messages ensured that the surgeon in the nearest fort, Waterfall, would get the news immediately.

Corban shivered as he meekly submitted to a change of bed linens and a foot massage with the lavender oil.

Solona worked fast, and with an intensity he hadn't seen in her since the minutes following the shooting five days ago.

Solona applied a vile-smelling salve to his back wound and covered it with fresh bandages. She slathered a different ointment onto the nearly healed entrance hole in his side, just below the ribcage, and taped a single piece of gauze over it. She then placed a hand on his forehead. "You're still too warm."

"You're kidding?" Corban searched the floor with his eyes for his blanket, which had been tossed aside in the rush to treat his fever. "I'm freezing."

"I'll see if Lorna has any analgesic patches left." Solona didn't sound optimistic as she stepped to the door and poked her head into the hallway to speak to Thane and Rupert.

"I want to see him." Nikki was also outside the door, and she sounded determined to get past her mother's blockade.

Corban hastily checked to make certain the sheet covered his bare bottom before Nikki pushed her way back inside the room.

She knelt on the floor beside his bed and gripped one of his hands in both of hers. "Why didn't you tell me you were in pain?"

In his mind, Corban had stepped inside a bright spotlight. He'd always been able to sense Nikki's presence, but physical contact enabled him to hear her thoughts as easily as hearing a voice on the other end of a com. The mental communication took effort for her, however. Her Talent for seeing memories was an unusual area of telepathy, and she was still learning how to control it. With practice, she was able to sift through his memories and reach what she described as a "higher level of consciousness," which allowed her to hear his thoughts, but it usually took several minutes of mental effort for her to get there.

This time it only took her a few seconds to break through to his thoughts. *That was quick.* Corban mustered a grin. *You're getting good at this.*

Tell me about the premonition.

The grin vanished. *I can't. Not now. I'm exhausted, and the lavender smell makes my head spin.*

Did you see anything different this time? she persisted.

Corban couldn't blame Nikki for being worried, but he was too tired to think straight. *I'll tell you in the morning.* He gazed into her large brown eyes. They slanted upward at the outside corners, a remnant of her Latina Earth ancestry, as was her natural tan and thick black hair.

I'll expect a full report in the morning. Nikki didn't even look to make sure her mother wasn't watching before pressing her lips gently to his. *And you'd better beat this infection.*

I'll do my best. Corban couldn't keep his eyes open any longer and reluctantly said, *Goodnight.*

TWO
THE *UNITY*

Thane stood next to his friend Zhao Kaczenski on the top step of the temporary staircase. The Carpenters Guild had cobbled together the stairs to reach the airlock of the small, obelisk-shaped starship that had touched down on Vesta-Lambda colony's landing strip early yesterday morning. Its silver exterior was pockmarked from asteroids. A single word with black letters half a meter high had been painted next to the airlock: *Unity*.

The highest point of the ship, the nose cone or bridge, appeared battered. Thane had noticed the misshapen peak from a distance and assumed the damage was the reason for the ship's delay in reaching the colony.

"Darkness!" Zhao snatched his hand away from the door as if it were roasting hot.

"What is it?" Thane asked.

"No human's touched this door for at least six storms. You know what that means?" Zhao's Talent allowed him to touch any inanimate object and determine its origin. He could sense the names of every person who'd had contact with the door since its construction.

Thane had been straining his own Talent to hear inside the sealed craft. He tuned his ears for any signs of life, but there were none he could detect. The engines had shut down twenty hours ago, and the only sound remaining was a faint hum from some type of machinery he couldn't identify. He faced Zhao. "It means it's unmanned, at best, or the stasis pods have expired, at worst."

"Well?" Zhao's father, Kun Kaczenski, called up to them from the bottom of the staircase. He was flanked by Vesta's five mayors and other colony leaders, all eager to get a glimpse inside the *Unity*.

Zhao rolled his eyes at Thane as the two young men turned to face the anxious crowd of people who had just banished the Strays to Seventh Fort six days ago.

"No signs of life," Thane said. "You'll have to break in."

"After we get away from the landing strip," Zhao muttered under his breath.

Thane nodded, his expression grim, and led Zhao down the long staircase, taking care to put most of his weight on his right leg since there was no handrail. A misstep with his deformed left leg could result in a nasty fall. He was already recovering from a cracked rib and didn't need to add another injury to his résumé.

"What else did you learn?" Kaczenski asked when they reached the ground. "Where's it from?"

Thane noticed father and son were mirror images of each other—same height, same black crew cuts, although Kun's was graying, and the same mistrustful scowls.

"It's from Earth," Zhao said. "It left New Houston six storms ago."

Kaczenski's mouth stretched into a thin line. "How is that possible?"

"You think I'm lying?" Zhao crossed his arms over his chest.

"You've never heard of a ship going off course?" Pavitra Brooks, mayor of Lakeside fort, elbowed her way through the crowd to reach them. She faced Kaczenski with her hands on her plump hips. "Your son has a wonderful gift. You should listen to him. He has no reason to lie, and I, for one, believe him."

Kaczenski's gaze drifted to the unusual red dot painted in the center of Brooks's dark brown forehead, but he had no response. His expression reminded Thane of someone who'd eaten a lemon, seeds and all.

"Let's get the Mechanics Guild in here to open the airlock." Brooks turned to Zhao. "Do you know if there're any working laser torches at the fleet warehouse?"

Zhao shook his head. "They'll have to use power drills."

"Good luck with that." Thane tried to recall if any tools at the metal-smith shed in West Fort could be useful. "Ask Chaim Rajamani for some sledgehammers. The smiths have welding masks if you need some."

Brooks arched an eyebrow at him. "We need to open the airlock, not destroy it."

Thane shrugged. "Like I said, good luck. Zhao and I should head back to Seventh."

He started to turn away when Brooks gripped his forearm and peered up into his face, her expression somber. "How's your brother?"

"He developed an infection, but Solona thinks it's not serious."

"Corban needs to be in the hospital ship," Brooks said.

Thane exchanged a tense frown with Zhao. "No, ma'am. He can't be moved right now." *Nowhere near the landing strip, at least.*

"What about Waterfall's infirmary? It's only a few kilometers from Seventh," the mayor said. "He'd receive better care with Dr. DeKalb."

"I'm sure he would," Thane said, "but right now your fort is the only place Strays are welcomed."

Brooks made a hissing sound like an enraged purple crawler. "Your uncle did so much damage to this colony." Her voice dropped to a whisper so only Thane and Zhao could hear. "I'm glad Leighton's dead. I know it's a horrible thing to say, but—"

"Not horrible if it's the truth." Thane extricated her hand from his arm. "Corban and I know better than anyone how deranged he was. Now if you'll excuse me, Zhao and I need to get back. We don't want any trouble here."

"You've done us a great service," Brooks said. "Your friend Rupert too. I wish he'd stayed here. I could use his help to send messages to people in the other forts."

"I'm sure he'd be glad to help you anytime, ma'am," Thane said. "I can't promise he'd be willing to help any of the other mayors though." He spared a glance at East Fort's mayor, who was scowling at him and Zhao.

"I swear I'll do everything in my power to restore you to your homes. Vesta needs every colonist, including the Strays."

"Thank you, ma'am." Zhao started toward the bike he'd left near the edge of the landing strip. Thane limped after him, leaving the crowd behind.

Nineteen other starships, in various stages of decay, surrounded the *Unity*, each separated by fifty to seventy meters. The ships were parked permanently on the tarmac. The *Unity* had touched down in the largest open space, between the hospital and library ships. Thane and Zhao walked past the library ship, where, before the internment, they had briefly gone into hiding, along with Corban, from Leighton Abrams.

Next they passed first ship, known to the colonists as the Shrine. It was the closest ship to the wide bridge that crossed the Cold River. Thane studied the sealed-off ramp to the massive, silver, bird-shaped craft. Vines obscured the landing pods, underbelly, and most of the first level from view, but the sign carved into a smooth round stone at the foot of the gangway was always kept clear of vegetation.

First Ship
Dedicated to the
Vesta-Lambda Colony Plague Victims
Twelfth month, VA year 69
Rest in Peace
Danger—No Entrance

"I noticed your old man didn't say thank you," Thane said.

"I don't think *xie xie* is in his vocabulary." Zhao shook his head. "He's never said it to me in Common or Mandarin."

Thane noticed some fresh scratch marks on the Shrine's marker when he paused to adjust a Velcro strap on his knee brace. As a former apprentice in the Hunters Guild, he was familiar with Vesta's wildlife, but he'd never seen any creature near the landing strip. Even the vicious night terrors didn't like the texture of the tarmac and kept their distance. Zhao gestured for him to hurry, so Thane made a mental note to investigate the scratches another time.

Zhao climbed onto the seat of the bike he'd borrowed from Solona Zegarelli and waited until Thane was seated between the handlebars. It was fourteen kilometers to Seventh Fort and although it was mostly downhill, Thane knew it would be a long, painful ride over rutted gravel roads. His sore backside hadn't recuperated from the ride to the landing strip, but he didn't want to linger.

"I feel like we should tell them about Corban's premonition," Thane said. "Anyone on or near the landing strip's in danger."

"If they were willing to believe us, I'd agree." Zhao started peddling. "You saw my father's face. I could've told him anything about the *Unity*, and he wouldn't believe me. I'm sure it was Mayor Brooks's idea to summon me."

Thane made a sympathetic noise. "Uncle never believed Corban, even if his premonitions showed him good news. Corban told him he'd win the election, and Leighton's only response was to slap him, like always."

"It's hard to believe you and Corban were related to him. Good riddance?"

"Yes, but what a way to go. Does Nikki still have the sword she used to decapitate him?"

"I think so," Zhao said. "I haven't seen it in Corban's room, so I'm not sure where it is."

"I can't remember what she did with it after her father shot Corban. Everything was a blur as soon as it happened. I would've passed out if Jing hadn't been there to keep me focused."

"Speaking of Jing—" Zhao cleared his throat.

Darkness. Thane had been trying to avoid the topic of Zhao's younger sister. He berated himself for the slip. "What about her?"

"I thought you told me you're just friends."

Thane was grateful Zhao couldn't see his guilty expression. "We are."

"You spend a lot of time together for just friends."

"I've asked her to give me some space, but it seems to make her more determined to smother me."

Thane was surprised to hear Zhao chuckle. "*Mei mei* can be stubborn. I was fine sharing a room with you and Rupert, but she insisted that we're family and needed our own room down the hall."

"Since Nikki, Solona, and I were up with Corban the better part of last night, that was probably a smart decision."

"Yes, if you don't mind sharing a room with your sister." Zhao snorted.

Thane paused, thinking how to phrase the dilemma that had been on his mind for days. "So, do you want me to stay away from her?"

"She doesn't need me to run interference, and she'd probably give me a black eye if she knew we had this conversation. Just do me a favor and stop giving her mixed messages."

"I'm not." *I probably am.* "I mean, she's been upset a few times since the roundup, and I tried to comfort her, but I told her I'm not interested in anything more than friendship."

Zhao harrumphed. "You told her that? She'll take it as a challenge, not a warning to keep away."

Thane winced at the fresh stab of pain from his rib as the bike bounced over a rough patch in the road. "I'll try harder to discourage her."

"Good luck with that."

THREE
CENSUS

"Name?" Nikki made an effort to keep her handwriting neat and tiny. The six sheets of yellowed notebook paper were all that could be salvaged for a spreadsheet, and she had to make every centimeter count. She gripped the short pencil stub between her thumb and index finger, ready to write the answer under the *Strays* column.

Jing spoke up before the Stray could answer. "Isaac Nomura." She was sitting next to Nikki at the scrap wood table, stationed just outside Seventh Fort's latrines. Both young women were perched on tree stumps as makeshift stools. Between their uncomfortable seats, the warmth of Ilios on their shoulders, and the stench from the latrines, taking a census of the Strays was proving to be an unpleasant task.

Nikki squinted up at the young man standing in front of the table. His untidy, straight black hair fell across his small dark eyes, which were similar to Jing's, although his skin was a shade darker, and his face was narrower than Zhao's. The line of people behind him stretched halfway across the courtyard. "Hello, Isaac."

"Nikki." Isaac bobbed his cleft chin at her, but he only had eyes for Jing. "Why did you set up here?"

"We figured everyone would have to walk by at some point during the day," Jing said. "It's inevitable."

"We need to organize." Nikki returned her attention to the paper and wrote Isaac's name, wishing for the umpteenth time that she could alphabetize the list. *What I wouldn't give to have a working datapad right now.* "Guild?"

Isaac laughed. "You have to ask?"

Nikki knew he was in her guild. She wrote *Herbalists* in the next column. "Fort?"

"Waterfall," Jing answered for him again.

"Family?" Nikki decided to ignore their silent flirting and focus on her writing.

"Two parents, three younger sisters."

Nikki couldn't help looking up again in surprise. "Both your parents survived the Plague?"

"Yes, thanks to your mother."

Nikki nodded but was quick to change the subject. Any discussion of her mother's savior status made her uncomfortable. Solona's discovery of the native plant that cured the Plague sixteen storms ago had been a fortunate accident. The deadly disease wiped out half the adult population before Zegarellium was discovered and made into a vaccine. Now the colonists were divided into three distinct groups: Survivors, adults who lived through the Plague because of the vaccine; Normals, children who weren't exposed to the Plague or were born after it was eradicated; and Strays, children who were below the age of puberty during the Plague and exposed to it. The virus caused their DNA to mutate, making them immune, but, as a side effect, each developed a unique mental ability called a Talent.

"Are your sisters Strays?" Nikki asked.

"No, they were born after the Plague. I'm the only Stray in the family." Isaac sounded bitter. "The only one stuck here."

"Does your family want you here?" Jing's tone was full of sympathy.

"No, but my dad said he'd prefer this arrangement to a civil war."

"I'll second that," Nikki said. "Talent?"

"Long-range vision," Isaac said.

Nikki elbowed Jing. "Why didn't you mention this before the roundup? You know how much we needed Strays with vision Talents."

"I forgot." Jing shifted on her stump. "Isaac asked me to the guild formal six months ago. I haven't seen him since *Baba* threatened to cut off his ears."

"That's not what he threatened to cut off." Isaac grimaced.

Nikki couldn't hold back a laugh but managed to cut it short when Jing shot her a warning scowl. "Are you willing to use your Talent to help the colony?"

"I think so," Isaac said, "but what would it involve?"

Jing explained, "We need to convince the Survivors our Talents are needed to replace the worn-out technology."

"But you're not a Stray." Isaac studied Jing's face with raised eyebrows.

From the corner of her eye, Nikki saw her friend's cheeks turning pink. She spoke up in her defense. "No, but Jing's one of us in spirit. We need Normals to liaison with Survivors, especially hard cases like her father's."

"That makes sense." Isaac smiled at Jing. "I'll help wherever I can."

"Thank you," Nikki said. "Which room are you in?"

"N17."

"Last question—yes or no to renaming Seventh Fort Brida?"

"I've heard that name several times over the past few days," Isaac said. "Who's Brida?"

An unexpected lump formed in Nikki's throat. She had to swallow hard before she could speak. "Brida Vaughn was murdered by Mayor Abrams during the roundup. She was an innocent Stray, a sweet young woman with Down syndrome who didn't deserve to die."

"She was a martyr?" Isaac's tone was respectful.

"Our first and, hopefully, our only martyr," Jing said.

"Then, yes, I think we should name the fort after her." Isaac switched his focus back to Jing. "Could I sit with you at dinner tonight?"

Jing straightened on her stump, her cheeks going scarlet. "I don't know."

Nikki sensed an excuse in the making. Jing must have forgotten about a certain metal-smith apprentice she'd been cozying up to since the roundup—Thane Abrams.

"I'll have to check with Solona to see if she needs me to tend Corban this evening," Jing said. "He was shot, you know, and we've been helping Solona take care of him."

"I can tend Corban." Nikki sent her a mischievous grin.

Jing countered, with a stern don't-help-me expression. She smiled up at Isaac. "Maybe I could stop by your room sometime."

Nikki thought her excuse sounded plausible, but Isaac didn't appear convinced.

"See you later." With a disappointed frown, he stepped away from the table and another young man took his place.

"Name?" Nikki asked.

FOUR
WOUNDS

Corban shuffled down the hall toward the apartment, trying to put off the confession as long as possible. His heart pounded in his chest and a trickle of sweat ran down his back.

It's not important. It was just a notebook. Corban tried to soothe himself, but he wouldn't be able to rationalize the loss to his uncle. Notebooks were valuable because paper was scarce. He and Thane were allotted one notebook each per school year. They were expected to ration the pages as if their lives depended on it. Leighton could well afford to barter for more school supplies, but Corban knew his uncle considered anything he had to supply for his nephews to be a waste of colony resources.

He'd probably let us starve if the dining hall didn't provide meals.

The thought of food reminded him of Aliza, and a hollow ache filled his belly. Uncle had dismissed the nanny a month ago, and she returned to Greenfield to live with her family. Aliza Yarborough was the only mother Corban had ever known. He knew she wasn't his real mother, but she cared for him and Thane as if they were her own sons.

"Thane's twelve now so he's old enough to look after the both of you." Leighton had turned a deaf ear to Aliza's pleas to continue caring for the boys.

"I'll do it for free," she said. Corban remembered how her lower lip quivered as she stared up at Uncle, hands on her hips. He'd always admired her courage when it came to confronting Leighton, but this time her words fell on deaf ears.

"Pack your things and leave now." Uncle turned his back on the young woman, and that was it.

Nine storms wasn't too old to cry, but Corban was forced to hide his tears. His uncle had no patience for emotional displays. Corban hid in the woods just outside West Fort and sobbed, hoping no one could hear him. Well, no one except Thane, but his brother never mentioned hearing Corban grieve.

Thane was withdrawn and despondent after Aliza's dismissal, going through the motions of each day in a fog. He was old enough to remember their real mother, and their father, who both died from the Plague. Corban suspected losing Aliza was like losing their mother all over again, but he never saw Thane shed a tear. *Maybe he cries in the woods like me.*

Corban entered the apartment as quietly as he could, hoping to slip off to the bedroom he shared with Thane before Uncle noticed he was home. No such luck.

"You're late!" Leighton emerged from Aliza's old room. He had already converted the space into an office. Corban didn't understand why a hunter needed an office, but he knew better than to ask what his uncle was working on in secret, locked away in the room for hours every evening.

"Sorry, Uncle. I was tracking a purple crawler and didn't realize it was so late."

"Liar!" At two meters, Leighton Abrams towered over his nephew, his dark gray eyes like a gathering storm. His jet-black hair stood out in sharp contrast against his pale skin, which never tanned. "If you were out tracking, where's the purple crawler?"

Corban examined the toes of his bluedeer-skin boots. "It got away," he whispered, bracing himself for a slap.

He was astonished Uncle didn't hit him. "Only an idiot would be slow enough to lose the slowest land-creature on Vesta. Why don't you tell me the truth this time?"

Here we go. Corban felt as if his heart was trying to punch a hole through his ribs. "I was looking for my notebook. A bluedeer chased me and . . . I dropped it trying to get away." He took a deep breath before admitting, "I can't find it."

He hoped his uncle might show a glimmer of sympathy for the bluedeer incident, but he was disappointed, as usual.

"You left it outside the fort, you worthless Stray! You go get it, right now!"

Corban's blood ran cold. "But it's almost dark!"

"Then you'd better hurry!" Leighton shoved him toward the door. "Run so you can get back inside the gates before they close!"

He stared back at Uncle for one paralyzing moment, hoping he would change his mind, but the cold scowl on the man's face left nothing to doubt. Corban stumbled out the door and ran as fast as his short legs could carry him.

"It's dusk!" A sentry shouted the warning at Corban as he sprinted past the archway, exiting the fort. "Gates close in ten minutes!"

Corban was unable to articulate a response. He didn't look back as he raced down the gravel road. He knew it was at least half a kilometer to the spot where the bluedeer had lunged at him, and he also knew there was no possible way he could get there, find the notebook, and get back inside the fort in ten minutes. *I'm going to die tonight. I didn't even get to say goodbye to Thane.*

The last light of Ilios faded as he ran, and the blood-curdling growls of night terrors echoed through the woods. Corban reached the spot where the bluedeer had surprised him and stooped to search the tall weeds around the ditch. Fresh tears stung the corners of his eyes, making it difficult to see anything by the dim light of Vesta's stars.

Isn't my life worth more than a notebook? He stopped searching, overcome with a burning desire to survive this suicidal errand.

Corban looked instead for something to use as a weapon, but his only option was a fist-sized rock from the ditch. He picked it up and headed back the way he came, running as if his life depended on it.

Because it did.

The stench of rotting meat reached his nostrils a heartbeat before he heard the night terror's snarl. A large white blur plunged between the trees at his right and charged straight toward him.

Corban screamed and hurled his puny weapon at the creature's snout, scoring a hit. There was a surprised yelp, but the night terror paused for only a moment.

It was enough time for Thane to reach him. "Get back!"

"Where did you come from?" Corban gasped.

Thane positioned himself between Corban and the beast, like a human shield. A machete flashed in his hand as he took a swing at the night terror, but it lurked just out of reach.

The size and fur color of an Earth grizzly bear but with the features and predatory instincts of a timber wolf, the night terror lunged, snapping its massive jaws at Thane's arm. He leapt clear with centimeters to spare.

"Run!" Thane pivoted left, positioning himself between Corban and the beast again. He swung the machete, aiming for its head this time, and managed to lop off the tip of its left ear. This only made it mad.

The night terror rose on its hind legs and snarled its outrage, flecking both boys with foul-smelling saliva. Its echoing howl was loud enough to make Corban's ears ring.

"Get out of here!"

Corban wasn't sure if his brother was screaming at him or the night terror. Corban's feet seemed frozen to the ground. Thane shifted again to cover him. A nagging voice in Corban's mind reminded him night terrors hunted in packs. This one wouldn't be alone for long.

"Run, Corban!"

The night terror pounced, coming down on all fours again as it ducked beneath Thane's frantic swing and clamped its jaws around his left knee.

Thane's bloodcurdling scream made Corban's heart stop. Without thinking, he seized the dropped machete and hacked at the night terror's ears and snout until it snarled in rage and released Thane's leg.

The beast turned to Corban and bared its blood-dripping fangs. Thane seized Corban's arm and yanked him away from the deadly jaws. His brother continued to protect him even though he was badly injured.

"Get down!" Thane gasped.

Without hesitation, Corban threw himself flat on the road next to Thane.

A heartbeat later an arrow plunged through the beast's muzzle. Another arrow buried itself in its broad forehead. The night terror grunted once and collapsed in a heap, the portion of Thane's leg still clutched in its fangs.

Corban heard men shouting. Someone scooped him up as if he weighed nothing and carried him faster than he thought possible for a human to move. "Thane!"

"We've got him." The stranger's voice was reassuring but tinged with fear. "Darkness! What were you boys doing outside the fort at night?"

Corban couldn't answer. He was dimly aware of the echoing growls of other night terrors in the woods and the shuddering cries of pain from his brother. Their rescuers placed them in the bed of a truck and the vehicle was in motion, speeding back to West Fort and the safe refuge of its inner walls.

***

Corban woke with a start, gasping for breath and trembling. The premonitions were bad enough. Now he was reliving memories in his dreams. *Not dreams—nightmares.*

There were missing pieces to this particular memory, details shrouded by a child's limited perspective and the brain's need to block out terrifying experiences, but those gaps had been filled six days ago when Leighton Abrams held a pistol to Corban's forehead and hissed, "You should've died that night outside the fort. Worthless Stray."

With those words, Uncle's second failed attempt to kill Corban resulted in the fatal shooting of innocent bystander Brida Vaughn. Determined to succeed with his third try, Leighton took Corban to the peach orchard where he planned to reload his pistol from the ammunition stash buried there.

I was sure Nikki was going to kill me. I saw it in my premonition before I met her. Corban shut his eyes, recalling the expression of rage on her face and the long sword in her hand as she raced toward him through the peach trees. She raised the weapon in both hands, closed the space between them with one last stride, and swung the blade at his neck. Corban ducked at the last second, and his uncle standing behind him was the one who lost his head. Instead of killing Corban, as he witnessed in the premonition, Nikki saved his life.

Nikki. The thought of her calmed him. Corban's rare second Talent, his empathy, allowed him to sense other people's emotions, but around Nikki, it was stronger, more precise. It was as if their Talents had somehow merged, sharpening their individual abilities and creating a unique mental communication between them.

"Limited source telepathy" was Solona's unofficial diagnosis, but he preferred Brida Vaughn's definition of, "shared light." The young woman had seen something unique in their auras. Corban still didn't understand what an aura was, but he was grateful for Brida's Talent. Her advice to "choose what you want to see" had been the catalyst Nikki needed to work past her fear of physical contact and learn to control her Talent for seeing other people's memories. He experienced a pang of remorse as he wondered how much more Brida could've taught them before Leighton murdered her.

Corban shook off his reverie and looked around his small room, but nothing had changed while he'd slept. He was surprised to have been left alone even for a few minutes since the fuss over his fever last night, but he also suspected Nikki, Jing, and Solona had hovered over him all morning and that one of them would burst into the room at any moment.

He reached behind his left ear and rubbed the analgesic patch attached to his neck, just below the hairline. It was Dr. DeKalb's last patch. The break from the pain and fever would only last until the medicine in it was absorbed. Solona wanted to treat his infected wound with thyme compresses. Corban hoped thyme smelled better than lavender.

He turned his face toward the single window, which was the room's only source of light, and guessed it was almost noon.

Despite this setback in his recovery, Corban was eager to get out of bed. There were obvious barriers to this goal. First, he would need assistance. His leg muscles were weak from spending so much time lying down. Second, he was hooked up to a urinary catheter, which tethered him to the bed. Third, he didn't have on a stitch of clothing. As much as he wanted to stand, he didn't want to moon one of his roommates, particularly Nikki.

And the fever probably guarantees me another week in bed.

His stomach gave a loud gurgle, reminding him it was lunchtime. Corban thought Nikki or Jing would be in soon, bringing him a bowl of something watery to eat. The liquid diet was getting old. He wanted to return to normal life—whatever that was at this point.

Right on cue, there was a soft knock at the door, and Nikki stepped inside the room without waiting for a response. She had a bowl in her hands.

Great, more soup. "How did it go with the interviews this morning?" He shifted onto his left elbow, adjusted his pillows, and scooted back until he was sitting upright with the sheet carefully positioned to cover everything below his waist.

"We're going to need more paper." Nikki perched on the edge of his bed. "Jing and I recorded two hundred names so far. We'll get back to work as soon as we've had some lunch."

"Anyone with Talents like ours?" Corban noticed her hair was damp, and her T-shirt and jeans were clean too. *Lucky girl got a shower.* He didn't want to think about how badly he needed to bathe. The ice-cold sponge bath last night didn't count for much in the way of hygiene.

"Two clairvoyants." Nikki rested the bowl on one knee and stirred the contents with the spoon.

Corban was pleased to see vegetables in the chicken stock, even though he didn't like the flavor. *I've graduated from plain broth, at least.*

"But neither woman has distant-future dreams like you," she continued. "Both have visions that come when they're awake and show them the immediate future—something that'll happen within the next five minutes."

"I wish one of them was with us when we were facing down your father."

Nikki winced at his words, but Corban found the expression endearing. He'd come to accept the humiliation of being an invalid and now tried to focus on the time he got to spend with her. He had a nagging feeling it wouldn't last.

"There're many telepaths, but no one else sees memories like me." Nikki brought a spoonful of soup to Corban's mouth. "Most of them learned to use their telepathy to read other people's minds."

"That would've also come in handy at the stand-off." Corban took the spoon from her. "You don't have to feed me."

Nikki arched an eyebrow at him. "Feeling feisty to-day?"

"No, just ready to get out of this stupid bed," Corban said around a mouthful of soup. His taste buds didn't approve of the celery, peas, and carrots, but he was too hungry to complain. "Is anyone else empathic, like me?"

"Many, but none who can read thoughts like you."

Corban shook his head. "I can only read your thoughts. Our Talents work together."

"We share the same light, like Brida said." She placed her free hand over his, and this time the mental connection was instantaneous.

Your progress is amazing, he thought.

It helps to have a patient victim for me to practice on. Now eat your soup.

Corban grinned and dipped his spoon into the bowl. He studied her face as he savored his first solid meal since the shooting. Nikki always kept her eyes closed when they were connected mentally. It was as if she was beckoning him to lean over and . . .

She leaned back, avoiding his lips. *I saw that coming a kilometer away.*

He laughed but was disappointed when she let go of his hand and opened her eyes. It was disconcerting to be alone with his own thoughts again.

"No sneaky moves while I'm trying to concentrate." Her dimpled grin softened the criticism. "Tell me about your dream last night. Was it the one about the ship exploding?"

Corban's appetite vanished. "Yes, it was the same as before."

"No new details?"

He dropped the spoon into the bowl and shook his head.

"So we have no idea when it will happen or why?" Nikki knit her brow. "I think we need to tell Mom and anyone else who'll listen. People should be warned."

"I agree, but I also know how much the colony needs whatever's on the *Unity*. Thane and Zhao know about the premonition, but they still went to the landing strip this morning."

Nikki nodded. "I was worried until they got back a few minutes ago. Maybe we should wait until the *Unity*'s unloaded?"

"But what if there's something explosive onboard and stripping the *Unity* will set it off?"

"That's true." She grimaced. "We have no way of knowing. I was hoping you saw a new detail in your dream." Nikki studied his face. "Think hard. Are you sure you didn't see or hear anything different last night?"

"I'm sorry." Corban loathed his Talent and the stress it created because of the missing information. *It would be better not to know, to be blissfully unaware of impending doom.*

Nikki set the bowl on the floor and cupped his face in her hands. "I'm sorry I brought it up. I shouldn't be harassing you when you're in pain." She leaned forward and pressed her mouth to his.

A wave of complex emotions hit Corban's empathic Talent, but he didn't get a moment to process them before his brother barged in.

"You two should get a room!" Thane laughed as they broke off the kiss.

"We have a room." Corban was certain his face was as red as Nikki's.

"Which you share with other people, idiot." Thane limped over to the bed and draped a pair of pajama bottoms over the footboard. "Solona said you should get up and move around a little."

"Finally." Corban wiggled his eyebrows at Nikki. "I'm afraid you'll have to leave for a few minutes."

Her face was scarlet as she snatched up the soup bowl and scurried out of the room, pulling the door shut behind her.

"What do I do about this tube stuck in my——?" Corban pointed to the urine collection bag attached to the bedframe.

Thane couldn't stop laughing. "Solona said to turn the little valve taped to the inside of your leg and then you should be able to pull it out."

Corban grimaced. "I don't want to mess with anything down there."

"Well, I'm not going to do it!" Thane ran a large hand through his blond crew cut. The tips of his hair were white, remnants of a peroxide dye job, which had allowed him to sneak inside Waterfall disguised as an old man. "My job is to help you get up and walk around."

"What if I need to pee?"

"Then I'll help you walk down to the latrines." Thane placed a T-shirt over the pajama bottoms. "Ready to join the land of the living?"

"Just as soon as you stop laughing."

Thane made an attempt to look serious, but it wasn't convincing. "Anything for you, little brother."

***

"This is the shower?" Corban stepped onto the wooden pallet, which had been placed over the mud floor of the men's shower hut. A plastic bucket was suspended just above his head, held in place by a rope. A sliver of soap encased in a mesh bag hung from a hook at the base of the bucket.

"Just pull the plug." Thane closed the makeshift curtain on Corban. "I'll see if I can find a towel."

"Great." Corban moved with care to keep his balance on the pallet. He worried about splinters in his feet as he took off his bluedeer-skin boots, shed his pajama bottoms, and tossed both onto a nearby folding chair. He added his T-shirt to the pile before pulling the wooden plug at the base of the bucket.

He gasped as the ice-cold river water hit his shoulders, but he put his head beneath the slow trickle and soaped himself as thoroughly as he could. He tried to avoid soaking his bandages, but it was a lost cause. They would need to be replaced when he finished.

The bucket was empty before Corban could rinse, but Thane was ready to assist. "Sounds like you need a refill." His eyes were closed as he slid a new bucket of water into the shower hut next to the pallet.

"Thanks." Corban didn't have the strength to lift the ten-liter bucket over his head, so he removed the lid and splashed water on his body until he was rinsed. "I'm going to need—" A towel sailed over the curtain and smacked him in the face.

"Thanks." Corban was grateful for the chair. After being on his feet for only ten minutes, his legs were starting to tremble. He was able to dry and dress himself sitting down. "I'm ready."

Thane stepped into the hut and swapped out the empty bucket over the shower with the almost full bucket. He offered Corban a hand up from the chair. "You smell much better."

"I probably need a crew cut like yours if I only get to shower once a week." Corban threw the towel over his shoulder and followed Thane out of the men's latrine area.

"Be careful what you wish for. Jing's been eager to shave your head since the shooting. She thinks men should have short hair."

The courtyard of Fort Brida was bustling with activity. Strays were busy at the dozens of cooking fires, the single well, and the kitchen construction site.

"What's the status on the *Unity*?" Corban scanned the crowd for a familiar face. There were many he recognized from West Fort and Hunters Guild. He wouldn't be able to hunt anymore and could finally change guilds without his uncle's interference. Despite the physical constraints of his wound, the setback of the fever, and the primitive fort he was forced to live in, along with most of the other Strays in the colony, Corban felt free for the first time in his life.

Thane interrupted his musings. "They're working on prying open the airlock. Maybe sometime tomorrow morning they'll be able to go inside. Want to head back to your room now?"

"No, I want to rejoin civilization."

Thane laughed. "What you see here is as civilized as it gets, but I have orders to take you back. Don't want to overdo it on your first day."

Corban frowned. "Yes, warden."

They started toward the east wall. Thane kept a hand on Corban's elbow, ready to assist if he faltered, although with Thane's bad leg it would be more accurate to say they were leaning on each other for support.

"Thane!" A familiar soprano piped up behind them.

Corban detected an immediate shift in Thane's mood as they turned to greet Jing. She threw her arms around his brother's waist and gave him an enthusiastic squeeze. Jing was short, the top of her head level with Thane's sternum, and she had to tilt her head back to see his face. Corban noted she was careful to avoid the cracked rib on Thane's right side. He also noticed Thane didn't hug her back.

"Hello, Jing." Thane didn't sound happy to see her.

"Nice to see you up and about." She flashed Corban a dimpled smile but was quick to focus on Thane again. "I haven't seen you at all today." Her tone was light, but Corban detected the disappointment lurking behind her words. "I know you got back from the landing strip an hour ago."

She slipped her small hand into Thane's extra-large palm and beamed up at him. Corban was aware of his brother's discomfort and couldn't help but wonder why. Just a few days ago Thane had been spending as much time as possible with Jing.

"I've been helping Corban. I need to escort him back to his room. Solona doesn't want him to overexert himself today." Thane freed his hand from hers.

Jing's smile wavered. "Let me help you." She shot Corban an imploring look.

He didn't need empathy to sense that she wanted him to tell Thane to accept her offer, but before he could formulate a tactful response, Thane spoke up.

"Thanks, but I can manage. I thought it was your turn to work on the census this afternoon."

Ouch. Corban sensed Jing's disappointment. It was awkward to be stuck in the middle, keenly aware of emotions each was attempting to hide from the other.

"You're right. What was I thinking?" Jing's voice rang, with a false brightness Corban figured his dense brother could detect. "We still have so many Strays to interview. I'll see you later."

She turned on her heel and walked back toward the table near the latrines. Corban noted the tension in her shoulders as her short black ponytail swept across them with the force of a pendulum, her hands balled into fists.

He arched an eyebrow at his brother, noting his guilty expression. "What was that about?"

"Nothing." Thane took his elbow and turned back toward the east wall.

Corban snorted. "Really? Then why are you trying so hard to distance yourself from her?"

Thane was silent for a few minutes, long enough for Corban to wonder if he intended to answer the question.

At last Thane muttered, "Zhao asked me to stop giving her mixed messages."

"So you're giving her get-lost messages instead? That seems harsh."

"It'll never work out." Thane's tone was flat, but he was doing a poor job of hiding his own disappointment. "She's smothering me. It's for the best."

"Just a few days ago you were enjoying all the attention. You think it'll hurt less if you dump her sooner rather than later?"

Thane frowned. "I'm not trying to hurt her."

"Too late for that." Corban ignored his brother's scathing glance. "You need to tell her how you feel. She deserves to know why you don't want to see her anymore."

"When did you become an expert on women?" Thane opened the door to the east wall staircase. "After you."

Corban used the banister to pull himself up the stone steps. "It's impossible not to be completely honest with Nikki since we can hear each other's thoughts."

"The rest of us don't have that advantage," Thane said. "We have to guess what other people are thinking."

"Why?" Corban reached the landing and scowled over his shoulder at Thane. "Why not just say what you're thinking instead of hiding your feelings?"

"Sometimes people *do* say what they're thinking." Thane returned the scowl. "They forget others can hear them."

Corban shook his head. "You lost me. Are you saying you overheard Jing griping about you behind your back?"

"No, I'm saying I overheard her tell Nikki she thinks I'm wonderful." Thane said *wonderful* with the same inflection as *toxic waste*.

"And that's . . . bad?" Corban leaned on the banister to catch his breath and narrowed his eyes at Thane. It was as if he'd morphed into the older brother, giving advice to the clueless younger sibling.

Thane's face took on a pink hue. "She also raved about things like marriage . . . and babies."

It took all of Corban's self-control not to crack a smile. The need to laugh was almost painful, but he never teased Thane on the rare occasion his brother was willing to share anything personal.

"So let me see if I understand." Corban took a deep breath in an effort to maintain the serious expression on his face. "Jing thinks . . . she's in love with you, and you find that . . . terrifying?"

Thane rolled his eyes. "I'm not terrified—"

"You remember I can tell when you're lying?"

"She's only seventeen—"

"*I'm* seventeen." Corban tried not to sound defensive but failed. "So is Nikki. You think seventeen is too young to fall in love?"

Thane spoke over him. "She doesn't need to invest her emotions in someone like me, someone who's—"

"Someone who's *what*?" Corban knew where this argument was headed. It wasn't the first time the brothers had clashed over Thane's opinion of himself.

"Crippled!" Thane said. "She deserves someone who's whole!"

"Darkness! What's the matter with you? Are you basing your entire self-worth on your stupid injury?"

"She deserves better!"

Corban wasn't going to let him get away with the poor-me argument. "That's Leighton talking, not you. We both grew up hearing we're worthless, but you know Uncle said that to manipulate us. Don't let him live rent-free in your mind. He's dead! We're free of him! We have our whole lives ahead of us, and you deserve to be happy! Any girl would be *lucky* to have you. Stop feeling sorry for yourself!"

"What's all the shouting?" Nikki appeared at the top of the stairs, her eyes swiveling back and forth between the brothers.

"It's nothing," Corban managed after an awkward silence. "Just a misunderstanding." He studied Thane's red face for a sign of truce.

Thane's chin bobbed once, almost imperceptibly, although his disgruntled expression remained.

"Tell Jing how you feel," Corban whispered so Nikki couldn't hear. He turned to face her and painted on a smile. "I think I wore myself out the first time out of bed. I could use a hand."

She returned a wary smile. "I have two." She descended to the landing and put an arm around his waist, above his injury, and gripped his wrist on her shoulder with her free hand. "Lean on me."

Although he expected to be bombarded with questions in her mind, Nikki's thoughts were quiet. Her emotions were complex, however, but he couldn't analyze them while his own thoughts were focused on his brother.

Thane didn't follow them to the second floor but went back down to the courtyard, without another word. Corban hoped he would take his advice to heart.

"I'm going to need new bandages," he told Nikki. "They got wet in the shower."

"No problem."

She half-carried him down the hall to his room. Corban didn't need her assistance, but he had no intention of letting her go.

FIVE
INVENTORY

The Unity's airlock is almost open. Rupert's voice in Thane's mind was tinged with excitement. *They're assembling a tech and medical team to go inside, and Solona wants you near the landing strip so you can eavesdrop.*

Thane set down the hatchet he was using to trim branches from tree limbs outside the gates of Fort Brida. He was working alongside six other Strays who were splitting firewood. He wished he had a way to ask Rupert for more information.

As if his friend could read his mind, Rupert sent another message. *She wants to report to you what's inside. She's afraid other members of the team won't be honest about their findings, especially if there are any resources that should go to the Strays.*

That makes sense. Thane wiped the sweat from his brow and nodded to a younger man, who was stacking the split wood into a pile. "Here, take my hatchet. There's something else I need to do."

Thane limped through the open gates and spoke to Derek Graham at the sentry station. Nikki's brother-in-law was Fort Brida's self-appointed head of security, although Thane thought the man needed to take himself, Nikki's sister Eliana, and their infant son Travis back to Lakeside. "Please let Solona know I'm on my way to the landing strip."

Derek ran a hand over his coarse black crew cut and leaned back on the tree stump he was using for a seat. "Rupert already told me why she needs you there." He tore a blank page from the dog-eared book he was reading and dug a pencil stub from the recesses of a hip pocket. "You'll need something to write on, and you should take someone with you for safety."

"Survivors don't want us leaving the fort?" Thane pocketed the paper and pencil.

Derek shrugged. "I think they're too excited about the *Unity* to care, but there's always a chance you'll run into some idiot, like your uncle, with a grudge and a gun. Better to be safe."

Thane grimaced at the mention of Leighton. He nodded a curt thanks to Derek and headed across the courtyard toward the east wall.

The stone foundation for the communal kitchen was coming along, although progress was slow with only eight donated shovels and two truckloads of stones delivered so far from the quarry. Thane scanned the crowd for a familiar face, like Zhao's.

He spotted Jing helping a pregnant woman fill a bucket at the well. Asking her to go would be an obvious choice—no Survivor would object to a Normal being at the landing strip—but he knew she would misinterpret the invitation as something more. He searched for someone else.

He saw Nikki talking to Dagmar Piroux. Dagmar stirred a pot of stew suspended over her fire pit. As he headed their way, he tuned his ears to hear what they were discussing.

"Whether the other forts want to help us or not, we're still members of the colony and deserve representation," Dagmar was saying. "We need to elect a mayor and community council as soon as possible."

"You say that like we're planning to stay here permanently," Nikki said.

"Aw, you miss your nice warm bed?" Dagmar chuckled.

"Um, yes. Don't you?"

"Since the roundup, I've been cooking three meals a day, over an open fire, with whatever Mom manages to deliver here—what do you think?" Dagmar's mother, Gina Piroux, was Cooks Guild master.

"I hear men find smoke-scented hair attractive." Nikki laughed.

"Cavemen, maybe." Dagmar snorted.

Thane reached Nikki's side. "Good morning. Would either of you care to go to the landing strip with me?"

"You don't want to ask Jing?" Nikki eyed him warily, but her tone was casual. Thane assumed she hadn't mentioned Corban's premonition to Dagmar. "No, on second thought, don't ask her. I don't want either of you anywhere near the landing strip."

"Your mom's going inside the *Unity* with the exploration team," Thane said.

Nikki gasped. "She can't! Has she lost her mind?"

"She doesn't know." Thane noted Dagmar's puzzled frown. "No one does."

"Doesn't know what?" Dagmar asked.

Nikki exchanged raised eyebrows with Thane before turning to face Dagmar again. "Doesn't know it's not safe for Strays to leave the fort."

Thane studied Dagmar's dark brown face to gauge whether she bought the lie.

She didn't. "Fine, keep your little secret." Dagmar swiped the back of her wrist across her forehead to push the frizzy black ringlets out of her eyes. "But if you know something the others Strays don't, something that affects everyone, you have a moral obligation to share it, especially if you're going to be our mayor."

Thane's jaw dropped. "Who said I was going to be mayor?"

Dagmar flashed a wicked grin. "I did. I think you'd be perfect for the job."

"I do too," Nikki said before Thane could get a word in.

"There are plenty of Strays older and wiser than me."

"Older, yes. Wiser is debatable." Dagmar turned her attention back to the stew. "You lived with the enemy for most of your life, the man who spearheaded this internment. You're smarter than you give yourself credit for."

Thane was spared from a guilt trip by Nikki's announcement, "I'll go with you." She turned to face him. "Let me tell Jing to check on Corban."

"If you tell her where we're going, she'll insist on joining us."

Nikki pondered this, her expression conflicted. "Fine, I'll tell her when we get back. I'll ask Derek to have Zhao check on Corban."

"Sounds like a plan. Let's go." Thane nodded to Dagmar and turned back toward the gates.

"Bye, Dagmar." Nikki fell into step beside Thane without another word.

Thane tuned his ears in Jing's direction instead of looking her way, which might catch her attention. She was talking to the woman at the well about Robin Aziz's new baby. *Good, she's distracted.* He knew he needed to take Corban's advice and talk to Jing about his feelings, but he suspected it wouldn't go over well. A lifetime of abuse from Leighton Abrams had instilled in Thane a habit of avoiding confrontation. Ignoring Jing seemed to be a less painful way to send the message that they should stop seeing each other.

But you don't want to stop seeing her, you coward.

He and Nikki reached Derek at the gates.

"Please tell Zhao to check on Corban while I'm gone," Nikki said.

"You got it." Derek eyed his sister-in-law with concern before stepping inside the closet-sized sentry station and emerging a moment later with her sword. "Take this." He extended the hilt to Nikki. "Just in case."

She frowned but accepted the weapon without comment. Thane smothered an objection when he noted how comfortable she was with the heavy blade. Nikki placed the sword through the belt loop on her left hip, the cross guard holding it in place like a makeshift scabbard. He had never mentioned to Nikki that he forged the blade for Leighton as a birthday gift. It was ironic that his uncle had been killed with his own weapon. Thane considered it poetic justice for Brida Vaughn's murder. *He would've killed Corban too if Nikki hadn't reached them in time.*

"Is there a bike we can use?" Nikki asked Derek.

Derek jerked a thumb toward the group of wood splitters. "No, but if you step outside, you'll see a truck headed to Lakeside in five minutes. You could catch a ride to the bridge."

"Even better." Thane hated being dependent on other people for bike rides, but his bad leg made it impossible to peddle. Plus, biking uphill with his one hundred kilos seated on the handlebars was hard work, even for another strong metal-smith like Rupert. He was relieved Nikki wouldn't be getting the workout of her life.

He followed her over to the electric truck, its paint job more rust than purple. *Cooks Gu ld* was visible on the driver's side door in faded black letters. The wood-splitting crew had finished filling the bed with logs—a fair exchange for a truckload of food—and the driver was preparing to leave.

Nikki hurried to the driver's window. "Mr. Bjoeren, could we ride back with you?"

The chubby driver was wearing a faded navy blue sentry's uniform. His eyes widened as he seemed to recognize Nikki, but his frown didn't budge. He peered at Thane over her shoulder. "I guess so. Mayor Brooks said I should assist the Strays any way I can."

"Thank you." Nikki moved around to the passenger's side door. "Just drop us off at the wide bridge." She removed the sword from her belt loop and held it in her left hand so she could slide over to the middle of the threadbare seat. Thane climbed in after her and pulled the door shut.

Nikki drew in a sharp breath as their hips and elbows were wedged together in the tiny space, but Thane didn't have any room to scoot over. "Sorry." He recalled that Nikki's Talent for seeing memories was triggered by physical contact.

"Don't worry about it. I can manage," she whispered, squeezing her eyes shut.

Bjoeren ignored their exchange as he put the truck in gear and pulled away from Fort Brida.

Thane turned to look out his window so he wouldn't have to witness the tortured expression on Nikki's face. "Are you sure you're all right?"

"I'm fine." She didn't sound fine, but he didn't press the issue.

***

"Let's stay out of sight." Nikki pointed to the weed-filled embankment next to the bridge. "Can you climb down?"

Thane eyed the slope with misgiving, but nodded.

They worked their way downhill to the riverbank and found some boulders to sit on. The swift current of the Cold River was noisy, but Thane was able to tune out the sound. He drew the paper and pencil from his pocket and handed them to her. "You should record what I hear."

Nikki nodded and smoothed the paper flat on her thigh. "It's not much room to write, but I'll do my best. Whenever you're ready."

Thane shut his eyes and focused on the excited murmur of voices on the tarmac. He filtered out the high-pitched whine of drills powering through solid steel. It took him a moment to locate Solona Zegarelli's voice.

"'I appreciate your concern, but the surgical masks will be fine. If the air's bad we won't get far anyway.' That's your mom.

"'Let's give it a few minutes to air out, just to be safe.' Jing's dad.

43

"'Ten minutes, no more.' Mayor Mariposa Savoy, East Fort." Thane recalled hearing her voice before. Her condescending tone was easy to recognize.

"'Be quiet and put a mask on, Mari. Don't forget the only reason we're letting you inside with the first team is because you claim to have some technical qualifications.' Your mom again."

Nikki snorted.

Thane winced as the drilling stopped and a sharp, grating, metallic shriek took its place, followed by a pop and brief whoosh of escaping air. Cheering and applause erupted from the crowd, loud enough for Nikki to hear with her own ears.

"That's it. The ship's open, and now they'll wait a few minutes for it to air out," Thane said. "Nothing to report except some excited muttering.

"'The surgical mask is perfect.'" He realized Solona's whisper was for his benefit. "'No one can see my lips move.'"

"She's going to tell us everything," Nikki said, "and we'll have a record of it. I've never admitted this, but Mom's probably the wisest person in the colony."

"I think so too." Thane kept his eyes shut, wishing he could see everything he was about to hear.

"'Here I go,' Thane repeated Solona's whisper. 'I'm two steps behind Jonah DeKalb. No lights are working so we're turning on headlamps.'" He heard muffled footsteps on metal. "'The dust is thick, so the air hasn't been circulating. Normally the AI would keep the atmosphere breathable, but all the monitors I'm seeing say every system's offline.'"

"I wonder how the *Unity* got here if everything's offline," Nikki said.

Thane shook his head. "No idea. 'Here's the AI.' That's Mayor DeKalb's voice. He's a mechanic. 'Plugged into the recharging station, but it's unresponsive.'

"'Jing's father: 'It should contain a complete ship's log. We need to hear what it recorded.'

"'We'll take it to Waterfall and let the technicians take it apart. Let's move on.' That's Solona."

Thane heard a soft metallic squeak. "'The ladder seems secure'—DeKalb, 'but let's ascend one at a time to be safe.'

"'After you, Jonah'—Solona. 'The next level should contain the stasis pods.'"

Nikki blew out a nervous breath.

Fading footsteps echoed on ladder rungs.

"'Who wants to go next? Kun? Mari?'

"'No, go ahead.' That's Mayor Savoy. She sounds scared."

"She should be," Nikki hissed.

Thane heard Solona climb. Then he heard heavy breathing—he assumed it was DeKalb's—and a soft gasp from Nikki's mother. Her voice trembled as she reported, "'There are . . . twenty pods. Red lights on each of them.'" She raised her voice to address Waterfall's mayor. "'These are different from the pods on the last ship, so the technology is newer, but the red lights are obvious. I don't think we should attempt to open one yet. We don't know how decomposed they'll be.'

"'Darkness!' That's Kaczenski. 'How long have they been like this? What happened here?'

"'Zhao would be able to tell us. Too bad some people don't think Talents are useful.'"

"The old bigot walked right into that one." Nikki scoffed.

Thane nodded. "He's sputtering, but Solona's speaking over him. 'Let's move on and see if anything can be salvaged. Next level should contain the embryo vault.'

"Embryos?" An icy knot formed in Thane's stomach. "How does she know so much about the *Unity*?"

"She reads a lot," Nikki said. "And she was in charge of dismantling the last supply ship, sixteen storms ago. That ship is now the hospital."

"She should be Fort Brida's mayor," Thane muttered. "I can't believe anyone would seriously consider me for the job."

"Mom hates politics. She'd say we should be represented by Strays, not Survivors or Normals, and I'd agree with her."

Thane was spared from further debate by Solona's whisper, "'We've reached the next level.'

"'Something could have survived.' Jing's dad. 'If the chambers stayed cold enough, some of the embryos might be viable.'

"'Darkness! Don't open the door!' And that's Savoy."

Thane heard metal scraping metal. This was followed by a gasp from one of the women.

Savoy choked and coughed. "'Idiot! The smell alone could've killed us! What do you think you're doing?'

"'Calm down.' Your mom sounds annoyed. 'There's no stench worse than a night terror in here. The power's been off so long, everything's dried out.'

"'I think I'm going to vomit!'"

Solona spoke over the temperamental mayor. "'Let's see what might have been.' Thane heard footsteps and her next words echoed, due to the tiny size of the room. 'Each section is labeled. Sheep, cows, horses, dogs, chickens, goats, rabbits, pigs, turkeys—obviously farm animals in this chamber.'

"'We haven't had dogs since the Plague wiped them out'—DeKalb. 'And we really need horses now that the vehicles are on life support.'"

Thane heard another door open and more footsteps. "'Humans in here.'" Solona spoke in a hushed voice. "'Looks like two hundred potential colonists will never breathe Vesta's air.'" Her next words were so soft, Thane wondered if he heard right. "'It's my fault we'll be extinct in one generation. We desperately needed these babies.'"

"What did she say?" Nikki whispered.

Thane shook his head. He didn't want to speculate, so he continued his report. "They're opening the third freezer."

"'Blood, at least one hundred liters of it; human organs including skin for transplants; organic limb, eye, and joint prosthetics.'"

"I'm so sorry, Thane," Solona whispered before continuing at normal volume.

"'Hormone replacements, saline IVs, and enough medicines to last us a decade—too bad most are expired.'" Thane heard a soft tapping on glass. "'The date on this morphine's long passed.'

"'What about the pills and patches?'—Kaczenski. 'Capsules don't lose their potency over time like liquids, and patches last indefinitely. There must be some painkillers we can salvage.'

"'You're welcome to test them.'" Solona sounded discouraged. "'Let's see if they sent us any tools and practical supplies. I'm heading up to the next level.'" Thane heard footsteps on the ladder again. "'What's in here?'

"'A seed vault'—DeKalb sounds happy. 'Most of these should be fine.'

"'What's in that room?' Savoy."

Another creak of metal scraping metal and DeKalb said, "'Solar panels!'" Thane heard him handle something that crackled like metallic foil. "'These are nice and compact too. They could easily power an entire fort.'"

"Those belong to Fort Brida," Nikki said.

"'Well pumps, water filters, light bulbs,' Solona whispered, 'and I'm assuming there are plenty of truck replacement parts in all these cases. Tractor tires and blade attachments. That'll make Elian happy—the slime worm.'"

Nikki snorted.

For the next half hour, Thane reported the team's discoveries to Nikki, who wrote them on her paper. A brief peek at her list revealed tiny handwriting, filling every centimeter of the page.

She read it back to him. "Kilometers of cable, wire, pipes, and waterproof sheeting; sewing supplies and bolts of fabric; bandages, sutures, syringes, vials, lab equipment, oxygen tanks; medical and dental tools; cooking utensils; paper, pencils, and datapads—I'd love to have one of those right now."

"And the ammo will be useful," Thane said.

"You're thinking like a hunter," Nikki said. "I don't think people can be trusted with guns anymore."

"A gun in the right hands is a tool just like a drill or shovel. Before the roundup, the colonists didn't use guns on each other," Thane said. "Besides, do you have any idea how hard it is to take down a bluedeer, with a machete?"

Nikki made no comment.

"Kaczenski and DeKalb decided to climb to the bridge. They're whispering to each other."

"About what?" Nikki asked.

"'Look at the size of that indentation'—Kaczenski. 'It's a miracle the hull wasn't breached.'

"'Yes, but look at the stations that were damaged: helm, navigation, life support'—DeKalb. 'No wonder all systems are offline.'" Thane heard the men moving around until DeKalb continued in an excited whisper. "'I've never seen technology like this before, on any of the ships. Whatever they used for fuel is very advanced. If I interpret this panel correctly, the fuel rods can be recycled.'

"Kaczenski sounds intrigued too. 'What does that mean?'

"'It means the ship potentially has an unlimited supply of fuel.'"

There was a brief silence, and then Jing's father chuckled in a way that reminded Thane of his uncle Leighton. "'We'll have to investigate this more closely, when we have time.'

"'I'll get my brightest techs in here right away.'" DeKalb sounds happy. I think they're done. They're all climbing down to the airlock." Thane frowned. "And they're arguing."

"Not surprised," Nikki said. "Let me guess—Kaczenski and Savoy want to distribute the supplies to the six forts. Mom and DeKalb want most things to go to Brida."

"Close. Mayor DeKalb doesn't know who to side with. I'm sure Dr. DeKalb will give him an earful if he doesn't agree to give Brida the solar panels, plumbing, and medical supplies."

"If only there were some unexpired antibiotics." Nikki frowned.

Thane nodded. "A dose for Corban would make me feel better." He heard movement overhead and looked up to see Rupert Conquist leaning over the side of the bridge, peering down at them.

"There you are. Solona wanted me to make sure you wrote down everything you heard."

"I made a list." Nikki showed him the paper. "It's the best I could do with limited space."

"It'll be enough to make our case." Rupert finished crossing the bridge and climbed down the embankment to join them. "They'll start emptying the *Unity* tomorrow. We'll need a delegation here to demand our share of the supplies."

Thane stretched his left leg and adjusted a strap on his brace. "That means we'll need to meet tonight and elect leaders."

"I don't like it." Nikki folded the paper and slipped it into the cargo pocket of her jeans. "It's too dangerous for anyone to be on the landing strip."

"We don't know when the *Unity* will explode." Rupert scratched at the peeling skin on his long nose. His Ilios-burned face matched his mop of auburn hair. "All we know is that Corban will witness it."

"Which means we have to keep him away from the bridge," Nikki said. "As long as he's in Fort Brida, we're safe—I hope."

"He can't stay in Brida, not with his infection," Thane said. "He needs a hospital."

"I agree. Maybe Dr. DeKalb will let him be moved to Waterfall's infirmary." Nikki stood and stretched. "How're we getting back?"

Rupert grimaced. "I came with your mom, on her bike. Mine's still at Waterfall."

Thane looked at the sky to estimate the time. "It's getting late, but we might be able to hitch a ride, at least to the fleet warehouse."

"That depends on who's driving." Nikki adjusted the sword at her waist before clambering up the embankment.

"Need a hand?" Rupert asked Thane.

"I can manage."

Rupert joined Nikki by the bridge and they waited for Thane. He tried not to show his frustration as he half-crawled through the weeds, dragging his weaker leg behind him to reach the gravel road. He was winded when he reached the top of the incline, but he brushed the dirt from his jeans and said, "Let's go."

SIX
ELECTION

Rupert led the way, glancing back every few minutes to make sure Thane and Nikki were keeping up. "I'm sure one of the food-delivery trucks will pass us on the way to Waterfall."

"Let's hope so." Nikki kept her tone light, but she suspected Thane wouldn't be able to reach Fort Brida by nightfall, not on foot. They needed a ride. She walked beside Corban's brother, matching his pace, which was half the speed of her normal gait.

"You two go on ahead," Thane said. "You don't have to wait for me."

"I don't mind." Nikki was at a loss for something tactful to say, since tact wasn't her strong suit. "You have nothing to be ashamed of, you know."

Thane looked askance at her. "What are you talking about?"

"Don't let your pride hold you back. So you have a bad leg, so what? You're no less of a man because a night terror took a bite out of you. You were protecting Corban when it happened. That was a very brave thing to do." She noted his reddening cheeks in her peripheral vision and curbed the chatter.

Thane took a few minutes to form a reply. "Did Corban tell you about that night, outside the fort?"

"No, I saw it in your memories."

"I knew we shouldn't have sat next to each other in the truck." Thane huffed. "Memories are personal. I don't like having my mind probed. It's like—"

"Like eavesdropping on a private conversation?" She turned her head to give him a shrewd grin.

Thane returned the grin. "I guess I deserved that."

"I'm glad I sat next to you. It was helpful to practice my Talent with someone else's memories," Nikki said. "I've only worked with Corban's, and it's been hard not to relive all the abuse."

"I should've stood up to Uncle a long time ago."

"I understand why you didn't." Nikki fingered the hilt of her sword. "I was able to locate that memory. The only time I've been able to concentrate on an individual memory in Corban's mind was when I asked him to think about it."

Thane shook his head. "I don't understand what you're getting at."

"I was able to single out one of your memories and examine it." Nikki bounced on her heels as she walked, unable to contain her excitement. "It was a real breakthrough. Normally I just get flooded with memories in no particular order, but I was able to fish that memory from the flood. I've never done it before."

"What did you see?" Thane sounded skeptical.

Nikki didn't get a chance to reply as Rupert, who was ten meters ahead of them, turned back and called, "I think a truck's coming."

Thane stopped walking and shut his eyes. "It's ahead of us, driving north."

A tremor of fear ran through her. "Should we get off the road? Get out of sight?"

The two young men exchanged frowns. "Maybe we should, just in case they're not friendly," Thane said.

They moved fast, ducking behind a large fallen tree in the undergrowth just beyond the ditch.

Nikki peered between a pair of dead branches as the aging vehicle approached, sputtering and straining to make it up the hill. A jolt of fear shot through her when the faded green truck was in front of them. She recognized the *Farmers Guild* emblem on the passenger's side door.

A glimpse of the man in the passenger seat turned her anxiety to anger. Her father, Elian Ramirez, kept his eyes fixed on the road, which was fortunate or he might have spotted Nikki, who was halfway to her feet.

A firm hand seized her arm, pulling her down behind the log. "No!" Thane hissed. "Now's not the time to confront him."

Nikki scarcely noticed Thane's memories invading her mind. "He shot Corban."

"I know. I was there too." Thane's blue eyes bored into hers as he released her arm. "Don't forget he's armed."

"So am I." Nikki patted the hilt of her sword. "I'm not afraid to use this."

Thane shook his head again. "Calm down."

Where's he going in such a hurry, with an empty truck? Rupert asked her. *He should be driving back to Greenfield or the fleet warehouse.*

As the truck continued up the road, Nikki whispered to Thane, "Listen. Find out where they're going." She studied his face as he squeezed his eyes shut, wondering why Strays needed to close their eyes to focus their Talents.

Thane listened for several minutes before replying. "The driver just said they should make sure no one's guarding the *Unity*. Ramirez told him, 'They're not going to leave any sentries outside overnight. As long as we get in and out before nightfall, we'll be fine. If it gets dark, we'll spend the night in one of the other ships and drive home in the morning.'"

Nikki kept her eyes on the tailgate until the truck drove out of sight. "The slime worm's going to help himself to the supplies!"

Thane stood and stretched his legs before climbing over the log. "I don't think Solona anticipated looters."

"They just got the *Unity* open an hour ago." Rupert vaulted the log and joined Thane on the road. "Ramirez didn't even wait for the inventory report."

"I wouldn't put it past Mayor Savoy to help herself too." Thane turned to Rupert. "Let Solona know to expect trouble."

His friend nodded, his eyes already closed in concentration.

"What should we do?" Nikki climbed over the log and joined them.

"We've got to get back to Brida and select a delegation," Thane said.

Nikki shook her head, staring at the spot where the truck had vanished. "I think we need to go back to the *Unity* and demand what's ours. If we're not there to defend it, there won't be anything left tomorrow."

She forced herself to tamp down her impatience as the two young men were slack-jawed for a moment, considering her proposal.

"That seems . . . dangerous," Thane said.

"*Crazy* is the word I'd use." Rupert frowned at her.

"Do either of you have a better idea?" Nikki kicked a chunk of gravel into the ditch.

"Corban saw the explosion. Hanging around that ship is suicide," Rupert said.

"Didn't we discuss this a few minutes ago?" She faced Rupert with her hands on her hips. "The *Unity* doesn't explode until Corban goes to the landing strip. Since he's still at Fort Brida, we'll be safe."

"It's taking an unnecessary risk," Thane said.

"So is doing nothing and letting the other forts steal all the supplies." Nikki rubbed her forehead, which was starting to ache. "You two can go on to Fort Brida if you want, but I'm heading back."

Thane snorted. "I don't think Corban would be happy to hear I let you face your father alone. Let your mom handle this. You know she won't let him take anything from the *Unity*."

Nikki scowled. "That'll be an ugly confrontation."

"It can't be uglier than the last one."

Thane's remark made her flinch as the image of blood gushing from the gunshot wound in Corban's side filled her mind. She nodded, too frustrated to argue anymore.

"We'll need reinforcements," Rupert said to Thane. "A delegation, like you said, to demand our share. Let me tell Derek to announce a community meeting tonight."

Nikki fretted. She hated being outvoted, but what they said made sense. "Can you hear from this far away?" she asked Thane.

He nodded, looking as troubled as she felt.

"Let's wait a few minutes. If Mom needs help, we'll hurry back to the *Unity*."

Thane turned and limped over to the fallen tree. He found a spot to sit and shut his eyes. "Solona got the message. She's organizing a group of bystanders to guard the *Unity* until dark. She'll spend the night in the ship and suggests we have representatives here at dawn if we want any supplies."

Nikki was appalled. "She's going to sleep inside with the dead colonists?"

Rupert frowned. "We need to have an election tonight? Tall order."

"We don't have a choice." Thane opened his eyes. "I hear another truck coming. This one's driving south."

"Let's hope they're friendly." Nikki gripped the hilt of her sword. "We don't have much time."

"I recognize Ms. Piroux's voice." Thane nodded. "We'll be fine."

***

It was full dark, and the gates were closed to protect Fort Brida's occupants from the night terrors. The courtyard was standing room only, and all the windows overlooking the space were filled with the faces of anxious Strays. The embers from dying fires and assorted oil lamps provided the dim lighting for the meeting.

Nikki scanned the crowd from the window of Corban's room, estimating that all eight hundred outcasts were present, along with the dozen or so friends and family members like Jing who had gone into exile with them. Nikki was envious of the two hundred Strays in Lakeside, safely sheltered from the misery of this internment. What she wouldn't give to be there, sleeping in her own bed in the comfortable apartment she shared with her mother.

"How's this going to work?" Corban was standing at her right, leaning on the windowsill for support.

Nikki clamped down on a suggestion that he return to bed. She knew he needed to move around, but she worried about him overexerting himself.

"You mean who's conducting the meeting, and how're we going to hear?" Jing was standing at Nikki's left, resting her elbows on the sill.

"Yes, that's what I meant." Corban extended his hand toward Nikki's, but she moved hers out of his reach.

"I need to focus. Sorry," she added, noting his disappointed frown. "We'll be able to hear because we have a human megaphone." Nikki pointed out the thin young woman standing next to Derek on the table they were using for a stage in the center of the courtyard. "Frieda Moul's Talent is unique. You'll hear in just a moment."

"Is there room for me?" Eliana came up behind them with Travis in her arms.

Nikki leaned over to kiss her month-old nephew on his pink, chubby cheek. He was being quiet for a change, even though he was awake. "Sure." She shifted left to give Eliana some space at the window. Corban wouldn't like her sister standing between them, but she couldn't spare the mental energy for him right then.

Derek was holding a lamp in one hand and Nikki's list of the *Unity*'s contents in the other. He turned to Frieda and said something. It was impossible to hear over the din of hundreds of conversations.

"Good evening!" Frieda's amplified voice filled the fortress, and a hush fell over the crowd. "We have many issues to cover this evening so I need you to please listen, and we'll discuss the particulars later, if there's time.

"I'm sure everyone's eager to know about the ship, so first I'll read off the list of its contents. I'll let you think about that while we go ahead and elect a mayor and community council."

"Tonight?" someone bellowed in astonishment.

"Yes, tonight," Frieda said. "We must have representation if we hope to claim any of the supplies. Please think about who you want to elect while I read the list."

Excited muttering broke out, but Frieda's voice was loud enough to be heard above the clamor. "The colonists on the *Unity* didn't survive the trip nor did any of the embryos, animal or human."

The muttering stopped. Nikki sensed the crowd's disappointment.

"But there are seeds, medical supplies—most of the medicine's expired, but the patches are still good. Truck parts, a tractor . . ." Frieda went on in her calm, clear voice for fifteen minutes, repeating the list as Derek read it to her. He had to squint to make out some of Nikki's handwriting.

"Now, moving on to elections—" Derek didn't waste any time.

There were some protests of "that's not fair" and "that's not enough time to choose leaders," but Frieda spoke over them, at Derek's direction.

"I'm sorry we don't have time for speeches and campaigning. We were forced out of our homes and guilds because we're Strays, so let's agree to trust each other. We need leaders who have the courage to stand up to the other mayors and demand the supplies we need and deserve."

The crowd murmured its approval.

"Let's have some names."

"Derek Graham for mayor!" Nikki shouted.

Her brother-in-law turned her way, with a frustrated frown. *That's not helping.* His voice in her mind was surprisingly calm. *Nominate Thane.*

Nikki didn't hesitate. "Thane Abrams for mayor!"

"I decline!" Thane's bass voice could be heard from somewhere in the courtyard.

The crowd laughed, but more nominations were forthcoming. "Angus Aziz!"

"I second Angus!"

"Fenton DeKalb!"

"Second DeKalb!"

"Jorge Zimmerman!"

"I decline!"

"Per Greenberg!"

"Second Per!"

"Dagmar Piroux!"

"Yes, Dagmar!" Nikki cheered. "I second!"

"I second Derek Graham for mayor!"

Derek shook his head. "I don't want the job!"

"I don't want you to have the job either," Eliana muttered.

"Linnea Savoy!" someone said.

"I accept!" Mayor Savoy's daughter called.

"Second Linnea!"

"Yasmin Wang!" Rupert said.

"I'm underage!" a voice in the courtyard rang out.

"You are not!" Rupert added a gleeful, "Second Yasmin!"

"You can't nominate and second, Rhubarb!" Thane's shout drew laughter.

Derek waved his hands. "Let's calm down, please! Are there any other names?"

The Strays quieted. No other nominations were announced.

"We have Angus Aziz, Fenton DeKalb, Per Greenberg, Dagmar Piroux, Linnea Savoy, Yasmin Wang—that's only six names. We need seven." Frieda turned to Derek with her hands on her hips. "You're the seventh, and you should be mayor."

Derek winced as the crowd roared its approval. He shook his head, but Frieda ignored his protests and took charge of the meeting.

"All in favor of Derek Graham as mayor, say *aye*."

The courtyard rang with *ayes*.

"Any opposed?" Frieda asked.

Silence.

"All in favor of the other six nominees as community council members, say *aye*."

The Strays cheered as the *ayes* were unanimous.

"Go, Derek!" someone said.

Eliana harrumphed and carried her crying baby from the room.

"Meeting adjourned!" Frieda announced. "Would the new council members please meet here at the platform with our new mayor?"

"What have we done?" Corban turned to Nikki.

"I think we just placed our lives in Derek's hands." She couldn't help smiling. "And I think he'll do a great job."

SEVEN
DISTRIBUTION

"If you wanted to help negotiate for supplies, you should've accepted the nomination." Derek scowled at Thane.

Thane returned the scowl. "No way am I qualified to be mayor, Mr. Mayor. You've got at least five storms on me, and you've already proven yourself a leader."

"It's too early to argue." Dagmar Piroux yawned from the driver's seat of the Cooks Guild truck. "Just get in, both of you. We'll need all the help we can get today."

Thane grinned triumphantly and stepped around to the passenger's side. Derek shrugged and climbed into the truck bed, where he was joined by Rupert and Zhao. The younger men had been hovering in the background, waiting to see if the new mayor would allow them to join the delegation.

"Anyone else?" Derek grumbled.

Thane scanned the quiet courtyard. Only a few Strays were up at first light, but they were focused on starting fires to cook breakfast.

"Wait for me!" Jing burst through the door to the east wall, still buttoning her shirt. She raced over to Thane's side of the truck.

"No." Thane held the door handle to prevent her from opening it. "It's too dangerous."

"Absolutely not, *mei mei*," Zhao said.

Jing said something unladylike and reached in through the open window to pry Thane's grip from the handle. "If it's not safe for me, it's not safe for anyone. We need the supplies, and I want to help."

"You just said we need all the help we can get," Derek spoke up, derision in his tone.

"Are we ready to go?" Linnea Savoy called from the driver's seat of the faded blue Medics Guild truck, which was parked behind them. Yasmin Wang was squeezed between her and Fenton DeKalb in the cab. Community council members Angus Aziz and Per Greenberg sat in the truck bed.

Thane bit back a retort as Jing yanked the door open and squeezed in next to him. He was torn between wanting to be close to her and avoiding her accusing glare. She settled his internal debate by grasping his right hand in both of hers.

"You don't have to protect me. I'm not helpless." Her whispered retort was filled with fury. "Let's go," she said to Dagmar in a more civilized tone.

The cook put the truck in gear and drove through the gates, exiting Fort Brida. Linnea followed close behind in the other truck.

Thane resigned himself to an awkward ride to the landing strip. He needed to tell Jing why they should stop seeing each other, but he also knew she wouldn't take no for an answer. Plus he didn't want an audience to what was sure to be an emotionally charged discussion. *Or a shouting match.* Thane wished they could hear each other's thoughts, like Corban and Nikki, but Jing probably wouldn't like what she heard if they could. He settled for silence, avoiding a confrontation altogether.

"We have a good mixture of career skills and Talents with us," Dagmar spoke up. "That should help with negotiations."

"I don't know any of the others." Thane hoped joining the discussion would reduce some of the tension. "Derek is Merchants Guild and you're Cooks Guild. He can send mental messages and you can make objects invisible."

"I'm herbalists." Jing's tone was flat. "And I don't have a Talent."

Thane squeezed her hand. "I think you have more talents than any of us."

She didn't reply, although her grip on his hand relaxed, becoming more friendly than possessive.

"Linnea is Tanners Guild," Dagmar continued. "She's telekinetic and a very kind, compassionate person, nothing like her arrogant mother, Mayor Savoy. Angus is in the Mechanics Guild. He's a math genius. Fenton DeKalb's with the carpenters. I'm not sure what his Talent is, but it has something to do with smell."

"Smell?" Thane asked.

Dagmar navigated a washed-out section of the road before replying. "Are you old enough to remember when the colony had dogs, before the Plague? They could locate things by scent, like lost sheep?"

"I had a dog once. Yes, I remember." Thane was startled to feel a fresh jab of pain as he thought of his lovable border collie that survived his parents by only a few days. The Plague had spread to Vesta's dog population, eradicating the loyal animals swifter than the adult colonists. Sadly, the Zegarellium vaccine was ineffective at saving the canines. None survived.

Jing nestled against his side, the tension in her body melting away. She seemed to know instinctively when Thane needed support. His sadness turned to guilt, but he didn't have the heart to push her away. There wasn't room in the tiny cab, even if he wanted to.

This is going to be harder the longer I put it off. I need to tell her. He didn't know what to say and hated himself for the emotional pain a split would create. *I should've kept my distance from the moment we met.*

Dagmar continued with her explanation. "So Fenton has a sense of smell stronger than a dog's. Per is Plumbers Guild, which is interesting because he can locate water like a human divining rod. And Yasmin's a nurse. I'm not sure what her Talent is."

"Rupert and I are metal-smiths," Thane said. "He can send mental messages, and I can hear anything up to two kilometers away. Zhao's a mechanic, although he used to be an herbalist before his old man kicked him out of the guild."

"Kun's an idiot." Dagmar glanced sideways at Jing, with an apologetic grin. "No offense."

"None taken," Jing said. "I agree with you. Zhao was a skilled herbalist. He knows more about Vesta's plants than me and Nikki combined. *Baba* thinks he can force out all the Strays and the guild will somehow survive." The tension in her body returned. "He's ashamed of his own son."

Without thinking, Thane slipped his right arm around her shoulders and pulled her closer. A fist pounded on the cab window behind their heads, startling him.

"Mind your own business, *ge'-ge'*!" Jing said without turning around. "I'm sorry I said so many nice things about him," she muttered. Her brother smacked the glass once more for emphasis before turning to face the back of the truck again.

The spell broken, Thane straightened in the seat and removed his arm from her shoulders. Jing shot him a disappointed pout before lapsing into stony silence.

No one spoke for the rest of the drive to the landing strip. Thane experienced a tremor of fear as they reached the wide bridge, recalling Corban's premonition. He closed his eyes as Dagmar drove the truck over the Cold River. He kept them closed until they reached the crowd at the *Unity*.

Dagmar blew out a breath of frustration. "This is going to be ugly." She pulled up next to a dozen more trucks parked around the base of the stairs.

Thane reached across Jing's lap and opened the door, but she slipped out of the cab so fast it was obvious she wanted to put some space between them. She glared at him over her shoulder before stalking into the crowd gathered beneath and around the *Unity*.

"Mixed messages," Zhao hissed at Thane as he climbed down from the truck bed.

"Temporary lapse in judgment. It won't happen again." Thane exited the cab, shut the door, and took in the scene.

There were at least one hundred colonists gathered near the staircase to the ship, and the ones who weren't arguing with their neighbors were staring expectantly up at Solona Zegarelli, who was standing just inside the jagged airlock doorway.

"We're going to handle the distribution of the supplies on this ship like *civilized* people!" Solona's voice carried over the crowd.

"Who put you in charge?" Kun Kaczenski shouted. Thane noted that both Zhao and Jing went out of their way to avoid their father.

"He did!" Solona pointed to a man in the crowd. "When he tried to loot the *Unity* last night, and I was the only one here to stop him!"

Heads turned to see who she was singling out, but Thane already knew. *Elian Ramirez, the trashbird who shot Corban.* Thane was pleased to see the Farmers Guild master slink away to the edges of the crowd.

"If the mayors would care to join me up here in the entryway to assist with distribution, would that make everyone feel better?" Solona called. "Equal representation?"

"West Fort doesn't have a mayor," Kun said, "because your daughter killed him!"

"She was defending Corban, as you well know!" This shriek came from Jing. "Abrams tried to murder his own nephew, just like he murdered Brida Vaughn! And you were going to just *stand there* and *watch*!"

Thane was pleased to hear a hush fall over the assembly, and couldn't help but admire Jing's courage. Some of the anti-Strays like Mayor Savoy and Elian Ramirez muttered to each other mutinously, but they were in the minority.

Solona sighed loudly. "Where were we? Mayors up here. Chaim, I guess you're standing in for Abrams."

Why him? Chaim Rajamani was Smiths Guild master and a devoted lieutenant to Uncle who assisted in the forced internment of the Strays. *Chaim will obstruct any attempt to send supplies to Fort Brida.*

"Coming." Lakeside's mayor, Pavitra Brooks, elbowed her way to the foot of the stairs. East Fort's mayor, Mariposa Savoy, was right behind her. Waterfall's mayor, Jonah DeKalb, joined the women at the top, stepping inside the jagged hole that had once been a neat round airlock doorway. Thane didn't recognize the mayors of Greenfield or Orchard Valley, but he experienced a rush of pride as Derek Graham joined the group. Solona's son-in-law glared at Chaim Rajamani as the guild master climbed the rough staircase.

Better him than me. Thane was relieved the burden of leadership hadn't fallen on his shoulders. He wondered how they planned to divide the supplies, but Solona answered the question for him.

"I have sixteen strong volunteers inside," she said. "They'll bring down items, starting at the top level." She wore a stern frown as she scanned the assembled mass. "If we can be mature about this and distribute supplies where the need is greatest, we won't be here all day, arguing over every little thing. Is that understood?"

"Yes!" shouted most of the crowd.

"Sounds good in theory." Rupert sidled up next to Thane. "But those seven won't be able to agree on anything."

"Solona will make sure Rajamani and Savoy behave." Thane squinted at the middle-aged, female mayors from the southern forts, Greenfield and Orchard Valley. "I'm not sure how those two will vote."

"We're about to find out." Rupert stood on tiptoe. "Here comes the first box."

The volunteer worker set a gray metal shipping box in front of Solona. She stooped to open the lid, looked inside, then straightened to announce, "Solar panels!"

"Fort Brida!" Derek said.

"I object!" Chaim Rajamani said. "West Fort's are wearing out!"

"So are Lakeside's!" Kun Kaczenski said.

Thane frowned as shouts erupted from the crowd. The mayors and Solona shouted down Rajamani, except for the sour-faced Savoy who just stood to the side of the entryway and sulked.

Rupert sighed. "It's only the first box."

"I know." Thane searched for a place to sit down and lowered the tailgate of the Medics Guild truck. He settled himself on the hard metal, and Rupert plopped down next to him.

"Move over." Zhao sat on Thane's other side, looking disgruntled.

"I just hope no one starts a riot." Dagmar shuffled over to join them.

"There's got to be a better way." Linnea leaned out the driver's side window.

Thane had an idea. "What about our Talents?"

Dagmar squinted at him. "What do you mean?"

Thane faced Linnea. "Could you move that box to the back of our truck?"

She stared at him. "Yes, but won't that make everyone angry?"

"Don't you mean angrier?" Dagmar asked. "What's the difference between taking the box and outright theft?"

"The difference is most of the crowd agrees that we need the solar panels," Thane said.

Jing wandered over to join the discussion. "The Survivors who don't faint will run away screaming."

Thane flashed Jing a conspiratorial grin, which she didn't return. "Let's try it and see."

This time Linnea whistled. "You asked for it." She climbed from the cab, faced the *Unity*, and shut her eyes.

Several people screamed, as Jing had predicted. Thane laughed as the box in question floated down from the entryway and settled into the Medics Guild truck bed.

The Survivors were either angry or scared, and there weren't many in-between. Savoy shot her daughter a vicious look, but Solona gave the group of Strays a thumbs-up and cheerfully announced, "Next box!"

***

It was late afternoon and all the trucks had been filled, driven to their respective forts, and returned empty for refilling. Both Fort Brida truck beds now contained a second load of supplies. Though there were still miscellaneous items left on the *Unity* to be divided among the forts, the Strays were off to a good start. Many boxes were claimed with Linnea's unique assistance, but despite rising tempers, no real fighting had broken out among the colonists.

"That's almost everything." Solona gave each of her volunteers a thank-you hug as the weary men exited the airlock. "The last items can be distributed tomorrow, but I need to go back to Fort Brida tonight."

"I'll make sure the *Unity* is secure." Mayor Brooks turned a scowl on Mayor Savoy. "And I'll make sure someone spends the night in the ship to guard it, even if I have to do it myself."

Savoy glared back at her but didn't reply.

Solona and Derek descended the stairs and climbed in the back of Linnea's truck. Most of the delegations from the other forts appeared eager to quit for the day, and the trucks went their separate ways.

Thane was thirsty and famished as he eased himself into the cab of Dagmar's truck. Although the temperature never got above 27°C during the day, Ilios's rays were intense. He could feel the heat on his face from being outside all day. He hoped Solona had some aloe in her medical bag. As he noted the pink faces on the rest of the Fort Brida delegation, it was evident that everyone would need some aloe gel this evening.

He looked over his shoulder through the back window, watching as Jing climbed up on the tailgate and took a seat on a box filled with toothbrushes. Zhao climbed up to sit next to her and they put their heads together to talk.

Thane turned to face the windshield. The temptation to eavesdrop on the Kaczenski siblings was too hard to resist, and he tuned in.

"*Baba*'s up to something," Zhao whispered.

"I know," Jing's reply was soft. "He and Nikki's father hung back the whole day and talked. I'm sure it can't be good."

"Rajamani joined their meeting a few times. All three of them seemed very interested in the *Unity*, although they didn't show the same interest in what was brought out."

"I noticed that too," Jing said. "Everyone else was demanding or pleading for supplies, but *Baba* didn't even look up when they brought out the seeds from the vault, and I know there were herbs in it we don't have."

"Ramirez didn't show any interest in the tractor parts, which was strange. I should've asked Thane to listen to what they were saying."

At the mention of his name, Jing harrumphed and didn't reply.

Zhao's tone turned thoughtful. "You need to stop pressuring him, *mei mei*."

"I'm not pressuring him." She sounded unsure.

"Relationships take time," Zhao said. "I don't think he's interested in getting serious."

"He's twenty already, past time to settle down."

"Says who? *Ma* and *Baba* didn't get married until they were both twenty-five."

Jing snorted. "That's because *Baba* ignored her for three storms, even when they worked at the apothecary together. Men are clueless."

"Hey!" Zhao said.

"Not you, you're not a man yet, *ge'-ge'*." Jing giggled.

"If you're trying to apologize, you're failing miserably. Rupert's twenty-one, but he's not ready to settle down."

"You haven't noticed the way he stares at Yasmin."

They were silent for a minute. Thane lowered his visor, took a quick peek at Jing and Zhao in the mirror, and realized both were watching Rupert in the back of Linnea's truck, who was in turn gazing dreamily at Yasmin Wang seated in the cab next to Linnea.

"Age has nothing to do with maturity and being ready for marriage," Zhao said.

"Why doesn't he talk to her?" Jing asked.

"Probably for the same reason Thane stopped talking to you," Zhao said. "He's not ready for a serious relationship. And you shouldn't be either. You're too young."

Jing hissed. "You sound like *Baba*, and that's not a compliment. You're only ten months older than me, so you can't claim to have more wisdom and maturity."

"But I am older and wiser, that's a fact," Zhao said.

"You're an idiot, and that's a fact. Don't make me shove you off this truck."

Zhao turned serious. "Whatever happens, *mei mei*, I'm always here for you."

Jing was silent for a minute. "We can't trust *Baba*. I'm grateful we have each other."

"Now give Thane some space."

"If you think that's what he needs."

"I do," Zhao said.

Thane breathed a mental sigh of relief, grateful he managed to dodge a difficult conversation with Jing. *With some help from Zhao. I'll have to thank him later.* His mind went back to what they said about the three guild masters who ignored the supplies and seemed more interested in the *Unity* itself. *What's going on?* He thought of Corban's premonition, and his imagination temporarily ran wild. *Are they planning to blow up the ship?*

EIGHT
SOLONA'S SECRET

"Your request has been approved." Solona strode up to Nikki at the census table and cut in line ahead of a dozen Strays.

It was nearing dinnertime, and Nikki's fingers ached from gripping a pencil stub all day. She and Jing had recorded the information for five hundred and eighty-six Strays on the spreadsheet so far. She squinted up at her mother, grateful for a free moment to massage a cramp in her right hand. "What request?"

"You want to go back to Lakeside, I asked, and Mayor Brooks agreed you and Jing should return and run the apothecary."

Nikki's jaw dropped. "You think we're qualified for that responsibility?"

"You two became the most qualified apprentices in the guild when Kun forced out Zhao. I thought Kun would take over at the shop since I've been here, but he's become obsessed with the *Unity*. He left Benito in charge."

"Benito? That idiot?"

"I'm glad you see it my way." Solona gathered up the spreadsheet papers. "I'll get someone else to finish the census. You and Jing need to go as soon as possible."

"But I don't want to leave Corban." Nikki wondered if her mother had given her this assignment as an excuse to separate her and Corban, but Solona's next words reassured her.

"I'm working to get him out of here too. Lorna DeKalb said Waterfall's infirmary won't take him, so Lakeside is our only option. As soon as he's stable enough to travel, I'll move him there."

Nikki couldn't hide a smile of relief. "Thanks, Mom."

Solona nodded wearily and turned to face the line of waiting Strays. "We're stopping for today. Please come back tomorrow, and bring any of your friends who haven't registered yet. It's crucial we finish compiling the census so we can get organized."

There were a few muttered complaints from those who'd been standing in line for a long time, but the group dispersed. Around the courtyard, Strays were lining up at the cooking fires for a meal served on new stainless steel trays from the *Unity*'s supplies.

Nikki stood and stretched. "How will Jing and I get to Lakeside, and when do we leave?"

"You can catch a ride to the fleet warehouse as soon as the men finish unloading the trucks. From there you can use my bike. If you hurry, you'll make it to Lakeside before dark."

"If we hurry?" Nikki glanced at the sky and thought what her mother was proposing would require inhuman speed.

"Go get Jing. Neither of you have anything here you need to pack since you're going home." Solona pointed toward the gates, where Jing was standing beside the Medics Guild truck, watching an assembly line of volunteers unload the back.

"You tell her. I need to say goodbye to Corban." Nikki started toward the east wall.

"There's no time!" Solona called after her.

"I'm making time," Nikki said over her shoulder before breaking into a run. She reached the second floor of the east wall, then Corban's room, and pushed the door open without knocking.

Corban was alone and appeared to be sleeping. His cheeks were flushed when Nikki bent to kiss his forehead, which was damp with sweat.

"The analgesic wore off," she muttered.

He opened his eyes and blinked up at her. "Nikki?"

"Sorry, no time to explain. Jing and I are going to Lakeside. I'll let Mom know you're feverish. She has some analgesic patches from the ship." She kissed him again, on the lips this time, and turned to leave. "I'll see you in a few days."

"You're leaving?" He frowned.

"Mom will explain everything." Nikki wrestled with a pang of guilt as she slipped into the hall. She took the stairs three at a time, determined not to miss her ride home.

"You're driving," Solona told Nikki when she reached the truck. The bed was now empty, and the volunteers had wandered away to find dinner. Jing was giving Zhao a goodbye hug. She seemed upset as she climbed into the passenger's seat. Nikki wondered if Jing's distress was because Thane was nowhere in sight.

Nikki waited for Zhao to load Solona's bike into the back of the truck before climbing behind the wheel. "Bye, Zhao."

"I'll see you soon." Solona nodded to her daughter and waved the truck through the gates.

***

Nikki waited for Jing in the empty hallway, next to the white-washed wooden door with *28E* engraved on the upper panel. The offer to help her friend pack had been politely declined.

"I need to do this myself," Jing had explained as she jiggled the key in the lock. "I need to say goodbye to the only home I've ever known, and it'll probably involve tears."

"What'll you do if your father shows up?" Nikki asked.

Jing turned away before Nikki could see her expression. "I'll tell him I'm leaving for good, like I promised." She slipped inside the Kaczenski apartment and shut the door.

Nikki leaned her back against the stone wall and gazed at the door on the other side of the hall. The name *Greco* had been carved below *29E*. She couldn't recall who the Grecos were. Even in a small colony, it was rare to meet people from different guilds unless they were neighbors or classmates, or unless the guilds worked together like the herbalists and medics. Nikki wondered if anyone in the Greco family was exiled to Fort Brida, but then she pushed the thought aside.

We're home, safe under Brooks's protection. I don't have to be bitter about the internment anymore. It sounded reasonable, but Nikki knew she wouldn't rest until all the Strays were restored to their rightful homes.

"Ready to go?" Jing emerged from the apartment and shoved a heavy duffle bag into Nikki's arms before dragging a second bag into the hallway behind her. "I took *Baba*'s luggage but he can get over it."

Nikki noted Jing's red eyes and refrained from commenting. She heaved the duffle over one shoulder, staggering a little under its weight. "Darkness! Did you pack every book?"

Jing didn't reply. She pulled the door shut harder than necessary, locked it, then dropped her key on the floor, and kicked it through the narrow gap at the threshold, inside the apartment. "That should make the message clear." She sniffled, shouldered the second duffle bag, and turned left, leading the way to the south wall and the Zegarelli apartment.

"Are you sure your mom doesn't want to move back?" Jing asked when they reached apartment 26S. "She really doesn't mind the two of us living here?"

"She thinks her skills are needed in Brida." Nikki unlocked the door. "Besides, Eliana's stuck there now that Derek was elected mayor. Mom thinks Elie needs all the help she can get with Travis."

The two young women stepped inside the small apartment and deposited Jing's bags on the sitting room floor.

"The herbs." The first thing Nikki noticed was how many of her mother's plants were wilting. She filled a watering can at the kitchen sink and went to work, dousing the soil in the ceramic pots that crowded the floor in front of the windows. Bundles of herbs were hung to dry from the exposed beam across the sitting room. She peered upward, appraising their progress, and moved to the cluster of tiny pots on the kitchen windowsill.

"Stuffy in here." Jing went to the bedroom to open the small window. "It'll feel good to sleep in a real bed again."

Nikki nodded as she went up on tiptoes to reach the geranium suspended over the dresser beneath the window. The red flowers were ready to be harvested, but she wasn't prepared to tackle that project yet.

Jing frowned. "It's seventh-day. Do you think we should go to school tomorrow?"

Nikki grimaced. "I don't see the point. I'm sure Mr. Gupta's already flunked me for missing too many days."

"We're quitting school?" Jing looked askance at her.

"I am." Nikki stepped into the bathroom to refill the watering can. "All the school-age Strays are in the same predicament. You're welcome to go back if you want."

"The Strays here in Lakeside didn't miss any days."

"The ones from the other forts did, and it's not likely they'll get to go back anytime soon." Nikki squeezed past Jing at the narrow doorway and returned to the bedroom with the refilled watering can. "I don't want to work for another three months just to attend a ceremony that says I finished. I think I've learned all Lakeside Community School has to offer. I'm ready to be a full-time herbalist."

Nikki could tell by the silence that Jing hadn't considered this. Her perfectionist friend didn't like leaving things unfinished. "You're welcome to go back to school tomorrow. Don't worry about me. I'll have plenty to do at the apothecary. Mom left Benito in charge."

Jing grinned. "Ben doesn't know the difference between lemon balm and lemongrass. I hope he didn't poison anybody while Solona left him unsupervised."

"I hope Kun had the good sense to check on the shop occasionally."

Jing's smile vanished. "You can't mention *Baba* and 'good sense' in the same sentence."

Nikki bent to pick some dead leaves off the marjoram. "Sorry I said anything." She glanced over her shoulder at Jing, who continued to trail her from room to room like a lost lamb. "So, are you going to school?"

Jing hesitated before shaking her head. "I think I'm ready to be a full-time herbalist too."

Nikki was relieved to hear this. She didn't relish facing the abrupt transition to adult colonist by herself. "Let's unpack your stuff and head to the dining hall. I'm starving."

"Yes, ma'am."

***

Nikki slept until late morning, getting a restful night's sleep in the comfort of her own bed. Jing overslept in Solona's bed too, but they attempted to make up for lost time by skipping breakfast and heading straight to the apothecary in Lakeside's market square.

The Herbalists Guild apothecary was one of the few permanent buildings in the marketplace. Most of the other vendors maintained simple wooden shacks or nylon tents to display their ever-changing inventory. The apothecary was a more complex set-up which required constant maintenance. Since the Herbalists Guild was small, only a handful of people in Lakeside were qualified to run the shop.

Nikki and Jing stepped onto the wooden front porch of the apothecary. A blue painted sign over the door read *Apothecary*, and just beneath it, in smaller print, *S. Zegarelli, FNP, CNM*. Nikki pushed on the glass door but stopped short when she met resistance. The sign in front of her face said *Closed*. "It's locked."

"Why is it closed in the middle of the day?" Jing asked.

"Benito!" Nikki pounded on the doorframe.

"We're closed!" an annoyed voice called from inside.

"Not anymore! Open this door!" Nikki pounded harder and rattled the doorknob.

"Just a second, just a second." A thin young man in his late twenties, with a mop of greasy brown hair and a belligerent expression, shuffled to the door and stared out at Nikki and Jing.

"Ben, you idiot!" Jing snapped.

Recognition dawned on Benito's sullen features, and he unlocked the door.

Nikki pushed past the assistant manager, already in a towering rage. "This shop is the only source of medicine in Lakeside, and it needs to be kept open all day! What do you think you're doing?"

"I can't run it by myself." Benito folded his arms in a huff and stared down his nose at Nikki. "Your mom's been gone all week."

"Looks like you haven't been running it at all!" Jing gestured to the long display counter, which was covered with haphazard stacks of drying trays and bottles of powdered herbs, many turned on their sides or missing lids. "This place is a mess! What have you been doing?"

Nikki didn't give him a chance to craft an excuse. "Go home. You're fired!"

Benito's mouth fell open. "You don't have the authority—"

"Solona appointed us assistant managers while she's gone. Now get out!"

"Fine, I will." Benito tore off his dirty yellow apron, threw it on the floor, shoved his hands into his pockets, and stomped out the door. "Kun will hear about this!" he said over his shoulder.

"Good luck finding him!" Jing slammed the door behind him.

"Darkness. We'll have to go through the entire inventory. It looks like the place has been ransacked." Nikki picked up the apron and was pleased to find the keys to the shop in one of the pockets. She then went to the counter and picked up one of the overturned jars. The label said *spearmint*, but she unscrewed the lid and took a sniff to verify the contents. "I don't know why Mom hired him."

"She probably felt sorry for him," Jing said. "You know she thinks everyone deserves a chance."

"He's barely qualified to haul garbage to the dump." Nikki took some deep breaths to calm herself and surveyed the chaos of the apothecary.

The five-by-five-meter room was flanked on every wall with floor-to-ceiling shelves. Glass canning jars of powdered and whole herbs, tinctures, compounds, teas, syrups, and salves filled every shelf. Smaller brown glass bottles of essential oils took up a bookcase behind the display counter. There were two rooms off the back of the shop. One was a compounding lab, containing a sink, stove, large work-table, and commercial dehydrator for processing herbs. The other was a small examination room Solona used to see patients. Nikki took the jar of spearmint over to the *S* section.

There were jars of dried parsley and elderberry syrup on the shelf where the spearmint needed to go. Nikki muttered curses under her breath. *This will take days to sort out!*

Jing picked up a drying tray from one of the stacks on the counter and started toward the lab. "I'll get started with the mortar and pestle. Where are the clean jars?"

"I think they're in here." Nikki returned to the cluttered counter and squatted down behind it to open one of the cabinets. Stacks of empty jars in assorted sizes filled the space. She grabbed a handful of jars and straightened, but didn't get a chance to carry them to Jing before a customer walked in the door.

Two customers, actually, and from their matching taupe complexions and unruly black curls, they appeared to be mother and daughter. The woman scanned the shop with wide eyes. She spotted Nikki behind the clutter. "Where's Solona?"

"She's not here." Nikki walked around the counter and approached her. "I'm her daughter. Can I help you?"

"No, I have to see Solona. Where is she? She hasn't been here all week. I need her to examine Portia again." The woman turned around and seized her daughter's wrist, dragging the girl forward until she was standing in front of Nikki. "Where's Solona?" Her voice went up an octave. "It's urgent we see her."

"She's at Fort Brida." Jing hurried to Nikki's side. "She left us in charge."

With a contemptuous scowl, the woman appraised both young women. "You're just apprentices. I need Portia to see a nurse right away."

"Maybe you should take her to the hospital, Ms.—?" Nikki kept her tone soothing as she fished for a name.

"Vandermeer. No, I have to see Solona. She's the only one who can help. She told me she knows why Portia's never gotten her period."

"Mother!" Portia's face flushed scarlet.

Nikki took a closer look at Portia and realized she wasn't much younger than her and Jing. She tried again to placate the mother. "Some girls don't reach puberty until they're thirteen or fourteen."

"She's fifteen!" Ms. Vandermeer said. "And Solona told me she'll never get her period!"

"Please, Mother," Portia hissed. "Keep your voice down."

Ms. Vandermeer's volume rose. "She'll never have children!"

A sudden flash of insight rooted Nikki to the spot. She recalled seeing one of Solona's memories. In it, her mother had been staring at a pile of bright purple Zegarellium roots and muttering to herself "long-term side effects."

And Thane overheard her say, "It's my fault we'll be extinct in one generation. We desperately needed these babies." Solona had been referring to the human embryos on the *Unity*.

Nikki was startled to notice Jing, Ms. Vandermeer, and Portia staring at her with puzzled, suspicious, and frightened frowns.

"What is it? You know something about this!" Ms. Vandermeer said.

"I'm sorry, but I can't be sure until I look at Mom's notes. It would be wrong to speculate."

"We deserve to know the truth!"

"And you will, in time. I promise!" Nikki shook her head. "It would be better for you to hear it from Mom. Like you said, I'm just an apprentice."

Ms. Vandermeer didn't appear satisfied with the explanation but made a visible effort to calm down. "Where did you say Solona is?"

"She lives at Fort Brida now, with the Strays," Jing replied. "She told us she'd stop by once a week to check on things here."

"Yes, we'll have her come see you the moment she does." Nikki shook her head again. "I'm sorry we can't be of more help."

"Come on, Portia." With another suspicious scowl directed at Nikki, Ms. Vandermeer took her daughter's elbow and steered her out of the shop.

Nikki waited until the pair was out of hearing range before turning to Jing. "I think Portia's condition is a side effect of the Zegarellium vaccine."

"But if she's fifteen, she was born one storm after the Plague. She never had the vaccine."

Nikki headed back to the examination room, explaining her theory to Jing, who fell into step beside her. "Ms. Vandermeer had the vaccine, all the Survivors did. No one knew anything about Zegarellium when Mom discovered it. It was never tested. The herbalists were trying to save lives before the Plague wiped out the whole colony."

She sat behind her mother's tiny desk in a corner of the examination room and tugged on the handle to the bottom drawer, where she kept the patient files. It was locked.

"I've got it." Jing found two paperclips on the desktop and straightened them out. "I used to do this all the time to get in the cabinet where *Baba* hid candy."

She inserted the ends of the paperclips into the keyhole and took only a few minutes to pick the simple lock.

"That's a useful skill." Nikki decided to be frank with her friend. "I think infertility is a side effect of the Zegarellium, passed from mother to daughter."

"What?" Jing gasped.

"Wait, let me see if my theory's correct." Nikki pulled out the V file and opened it on the desk. She sifted through the scraps of paper and yellowed index cards until she found *Portia Vandermeer* written across the top of a stained sheet of notebook paper.

Jing read over Nikki's shoulder. There was only one piece of information written in boldface: *no uterus.*

***

"Darkness." Nikki was glad she hadn't eaten breakfast because she would've been sick after reading a handful of files.

Jing sat cross-legged on the floor, sifting through the index cards in the C file. "Tovah Cartier, age twelve, no uterus. Ayanna Costa, age thirteen, no uterus and only one ovary. Mothers have been bringing their daughters to see Solona for storms, worried why they weren't getting their periods."

"Now we know why—the vaccine. Every woman who had it passed on this side effect to her daughters. Mom must be devastated to know her discovery caused this."

"It's not her fault it wasn't tested," Jing said. "There was no time to do a long-term study when people were dying from the Plague in less than forty-eight hours."

"I know." Nikki sighed. "I just feel bad she's going to have to tell the colony that Normal girls born to Survivor mothers will never have children."

The color drained from Jing's round face. "I had the vaccine."

"You'll be able to have children."

"But my daughters won't. I'll never be a grand-mother. You said Solona thinks the colony will die out in one generation."

Nikki was thoughtful. "No, we won't die out. Most Strays didn't have the vaccine because they didn't need it. And we have no idea how the vaccine affected men. Maybe the infertility didn't pass from Survivor father to Normal son."

Jing rolled her eyes. "No one's going to ask a nurse to check their son's sperm count. We won't know until they're ready to be fathers themselves."

"That'll be awhile. Normals born after the Plague are younger than us. It could be eight storms or more before we know."

The bell on the shop door tinkled, and Nikki and Jing scrambled to their feet.

"We'll have to discuss this later, with Mom. Right now we've got an apothecary to run." Nikki went out to greet the customer, who needed a remedy for a toothache. She was relieved to find the clove oil in the right spot.

NINE
NIGHT WATCH

"This assignment was approved by West Fort's interim mayor, Chaim Rajamani—"

"What?" Thane interrupted Solona's explanation. "That slime worm is—?"

"Relax, Gina Piroux is running against him in the election next week." Solona spoke over his sputtered protests. "With his toxic personality and active role in the forced internment, he has zero chance of winning." She cleared her throat. "As I was saying, Rajamani agreed to allow a Stray communication team to live in West Fort on a trial basis."

Thane shut his mouth and let her finish, relieved to hear his sadistic former supervisor wouldn't hold power over him for this assignment.

"You can live in your old apartment," Solona continued. "They removed your uncle's bed and belongings and provided more hammocks so two Strays can share his bedroom."

"Four of us?" Rupert asked.

Solona nodded. "You, Thane, Zhao, and Isaac Nomura."

"Who's Isaac Nomura?" Thane asked.

"Herbalists Guild. His vision Talent allows him to see long distances."

"So, he's like a pair of human binoculars?" Rupert asked. "But how does Zhao's Talent work with communication?"

"What about Corban?" Thane asked. "I want him on the team."

"Zhao's Talent offers a wealth of possibilities," Solona said. "He can identify evidence for any type of crime, like breaking and entering or theft."

Rupert scratched his head. "I don't get it. Are we supposed to be sentries?"

"Yes, as of today you're members of the Sentries Guild. Guild Master Athena Yarborough is sympathetic to the Strays. She lives in Greenfield but says she knows you and Corban."

Thane nodded. "She probably heard of us through her daughter. Aliza Yarborough was our nanny when Corban and I were little."

"We thought the sentries would be the best fit for your Talents." Solona offered Thane a half smile. "Athena agreed and was happy to accept you into the guild."

"What about Corban?" Thane asked again.

Solona frowned. "I know you'd like to stay together, but I'm not sure how his clairvoyance Talent could help with public safety."

"Maybe not his premonitions, but his empathy could be useful," Thane said. "He's like a human lie-detector. Between him and Zhao, people would have a hard time getting away with any type of crime."

"I'll bring up the idea at the next mayors meeting. For now, he needs more time to recuperate. Mayor

Brooks has approved moving him to Lakeside's infirmary in a few days."

Thane's jaw dropped in surprise. "You've been busy."

"I've been persistent." Solona shrugged. "The Merchants Guild is sending a truck here tomorrow morning to take you to West, so you might want to pack tonight."

"Pack what?" Rupert scoffed. "I've got one change of clothes and a toothbrush. Think our ride could stop by Waterfall for the rest of my stuff?"

"It depends on who's driving," Solona said. "I can't make any promises."

Thane nodded. "Thank you for getting us these new assignments."

***

"I guess we won't be seeing each other for a while." Thane stood by, ready to assist if needed as Corban shifted his feet to the floor and got up from the bed. Corban's face was still flushed despite Solona's assurance that the thyme compresses were clearing up his infection.

"I'm just happy we're both getting out of here." Corban leaned on the headboard for support.

"You'll start physical therapy at Lakeside. They've got all the equipment and a PT on staff. I believe she's one of Mayor Brooks's children."

Corban steadied himself and gave Thane a serious look. "As long as they're not sending me to the landing strip—" He didn't need to finish the thought.

Thane nodded. "I'll bring over your clothes as soon as I can."

"Thanks. I'm tired of wearing pajamas."

***

Thane, Rupert, and Zhao were up early, ready to board a Merchants Guild truck. The driver was a woman who appeared to be good friends with Solona Zegarelli.

"Here they are, Blythe," Solona said. "We just need to wait for Isaac. Thanks for driving them."

"No problem." Blythe climbed from the cab and hugged Solona. "It was nice to see Derek and the baby for a few minutes anyway. Travis is getting so big. How's Eliana?"

Solona noted Thane's confused expression and explained, "Blythe is Derek's aunt." She turned back to the driver. "She's fine. Tired of sleeping on the floor though."

"I collected some diapers and baby clothes. These are donations from my neighbors whose babies have long outgrown them." Blythe reached into the cab and lifted out a woven hemp basket filled with small pastel-colored fabrics.

"Thank you, that was very thoughtful." Solona took the basket from her. "Robin Aziz could use some of these too. I'm a little embarrassed to tell you she named her baby Solona. Ah, here's Isaac."

Thane glanced over his shoulder at the approaching fourth member of the team. He had black hair and small dark eyes, like Zhao's, but his face was narrower.

Isaac set his duffle bag in the truck bed and shook hands with each of them. "Rupert, Thane, nice to meet you. Zhao, how've you been?"

"I haven't seen you since my old man kicked me out of the guild. Leaving anyone behind?" Zhao asked.

"No, my family lives in Waterfall. I just turned eighteen, so it doesn't matter where I live now."

"Waterfall's not far from West Fort," Rupert said. "You could see them on your days off."

"Do we get any days off?" Isaac asked. "I was told I'm supposed to keep watch every night."

"We need more Strays like you with vision Talents," Thane said. "But the Survivors have to warm up to the idea of allowing us to use our Talents. West Fort wants to test the four of us to see if our Talents are useful."

Rupert rolled his eyes. "How generous of them."

"Too bad they didn't think of that before banishing you." Blythe scowled. "Ready to go?"

"Ready." Isaac sat in the truck bed.

Rupert and Zhao gave Thane a hand up, and West Fort's new communication team took their leave of Fort Brida.

"Good luck." Solona patted the tailgate as they drove away.

Thane braced himself for a bumpy ride.

Blythe Graham allowed Rupert a fifteen-minute stop at Waterfall. She drove across the hydroelectric dam and parked just outside the gates to the largest fortress, built on a high plateau overlooking Cold River's natural fifty-meter plunge. Rupert received reluctant permission from the gate sentries to visit the Smiths Guild barracks to retrieve his belongings.

Pushing his bike, he returned to the truck, with a large rucksack over his shoulder, and a lopsided grin on his freckled face. "I'll never take something as simple as a change of clothes for granted again. Help me load the bike," he asked Zhao.

It took Blythe another forty-five minutes to navigate the five kilometers of washed-out gravel roads to West Fort. They were met at the open gates by an older sentry Thane recognized. The nametag on her faded navy-blue uniform read *L. O'Rourke*. She frowned at

Thane, an expression that didn't improve as she eyed the other three young men in the truck, but said nothing as she handed Blythe a key and waved them through the archway.

"Should be fun working with her," Zhao muttered when O'Rourke was out of earshot.

We're home. Rupert sounded optimistic, but Thane wondered if they could expect the same chilly reception from other colonists.

"Not everyone hates Strays, right?" Isaac seemed to read his mind.

"Let's hope they accept our authority as sentries," Zhao said, "or this experiment will be a waste of time."

"Time, exactly," Thane said. "It'll take time to warm up to the idea of Strays using their Talents to benefit the colony."

"They had sixteen storms to warm up to the idea." Isaac snorted. "Don't expect a dramatic change in attitude, not after your uncle organized the internment."

The younger man's flippant remark irritated Thane, but he kept his mouth shut.

Blythe navigated the cobbled streets to the west wall, where she pulled up near the doorway to the upper floor's staircase. "All out."

They climbed from the truck, with their gear, thanked Blythe for the ride, and ascended the stone staircase to the third floor. Thane couldn't help smiling as he led the way across the hall to apartment 30W. Another door ten meters down the hall to the right was labeled *30W-B*, but for the first time since the Abrams moved to the apartment six storms ago, Thane didn't have to enter the suite through that door, which opened to the bedroom he used to share with Corban.

He inserted the key in the newly changed lock of 30W and stepped inside the spacious corner apartment.

"Nice place." Isaac sauntered in behind Thane.

The community council's large oval table and seven chairs had been removed, replaced by a smaller, modest table with four chairs. The night terror fur rugs had also been removed, along with the contents of the bookcase that stood against the wall opposite the kitchenette.

Rupert slipped past Thane and went straight to the full-sized refrigerator. "Empty. You'd think they'd at least leave us some apples."

Thane set his backpack on the table. "Try the freezer."

"That's better!" Rupert unearthed a container of strawberry ice cream.

"Let's hope it doesn't have freezer burn." Zhao crossed the room and peered through the doorway to Uncle's room. The other three followed him.

Leighton Abrams's massive bed had been taken away, along with the ornately carved wardrobe. Two hammocks hung from new eye hooks, screwed into the log walls, and someone had donated a derelict-looking dresser.

"Who gets to use this?" Isaac poked his head inside Uncle's bathroom, the most opulent space in the entire colony, with copper fixtures, a heated tile floor, and a large soaking tub.

Thane associated too many unpleasant memories with his uncle's quarters. "You can. I'll stick with my old room." He opened the door to the adjoining bedroom, and they all went inside.

The only thing missing is Corban. Thane was pleased to see everything as he left it three weeks ago, including the dirty clothes scattered over the hardwood floor and piled in corners in the simple wooden bathroom with stone walls. "Who wants to bunk in here with me?"

"I do," Rupert said, "if Zhao doesn't mind."

Zhao exchanged a noncommittal shrug with Thane and followed Isaac back into Uncle's former bedroom. "I think the first thing we should do is find some real food," he said over his shoulder.

No one had to second the motion. The four washed their hands and headed downstairs. Rupert, who had lived in West Fort before being allowed to move into the Smiths Guild barracks at Waterfall, led the way down the cobbled street to the dining hall.

Breakfast was being cleared away from the buffet table, but Gina Piroux caught sight of Thane and shouted to her Cooks Guild staff. "Leave the food out! These boys are hungry!"

"Thank you, Madam Mayor!" Thane picked up a plate from the stack at the head of the buffet and helped himself to heaping servings of everything leftover from the breakfast rush. After a week of burnt offerings from campfire meals, he was eager to taste Ms. Piroux's excellent rolls and pastries again.

"Not mayor yet." Ms. Piroux filled cups of apple juice for them at the far end of the table. "What's your name, handsome?" She offered a cup to Isaac, her toothy white smile splitting her dark brown face in two. Thane thought Dagmar looked exactly like her mother, except Ms. Piroux's wild ringlets were gray instead of black.

Isaac gaped at her before finding his voice. "Isaac Nomura. I'm from Waterfall."

"And you?" She flashed the same smile at Zhao, who had a mouth full of cinnamon roll. "Are either of you old enough to date my daughter?" she asked without missing a beat.

Thane had just taken a gulp of juice and promptly snorted it out both nostrils.

Rupert rescued Zhao by speaking up. "This is Zhao Kaczenski. He's from Lakeside. They're both younger than me and Thane."

Ms. Piroux handed Thane a napkin before tut-tutting her disapproval. "I thought you might be too young. If that girl doesn't hurry up and catch herself a man, there won't be any left to go around."

"I'm sure there're plenty of young men her age." Thane's eyes watered from the painful juice explosion. He wiped his chin and resumed filling his plate, ignoring the laughter from Rupert and Zhao.

"The only men her age are Survivors," Ms. Piroux said. "And none of them seem interested in dating Strays."

"Seems to be a lot of that going around," Zhao said. "Not many Strays want to date Normals either."

Thane shot him a frown before moving to a nearby table with his overflowing plate. *First he wants me to stop seeing Jing, now he's mad because I stopped? He needs to make up his mind.*

"Anything you boys want to eat, just ask." Ms. Piroux headed back to the kitchen. "Let me know if anyone on my staff gives you grief," she added over her shoulder. "I'll have them gutting fish for a month."

"Thank you, Ms. Piroux," Rupert and Thane called after her.

The cook waved and disappeared through the swinging door.

The other three joined Thane at the table.

"Did you eat like this all the time?" Zhao finished the cinnamon roll, licking the icing from his fingers.

"Yes." Rupert managed to speak, with a mouth crammed full of scrambled eggs. "West Fort has the best food in the colony."

"Because we have the best cooks in the colony." Thane finished his sausage. "Solona didn't leave us any instructions. What're we supposed to do now that we're here?"

"Just venturing a guess," Zhao said, "but we should probably talk to the head sentry about uniforms, training, work schedules, that type of thing."

"Who's the head sentry?" Isaac asked.

Thane and Rupert exchanged a shrug. "No idea," Thane said.

Rupert stood, with his empty plate. "First thing I need to do is see my mom. I've been sending her messages since the internment began, but I'm sure she's still worried. I'll stop by the sentry station as soon as I can."

"Later, Rhubarb." Thane nodded to his friend as he headed out of the empty dining room. Thane waited for Zhao and Isaac to finish eating. He leaned back in his chair and closed his eyes. Although he didn't intend to eavesdrop, a conversation in the kitchen drew his interest.

"I don't understand. Why were they allowed to come back?" one apprentice cook, a female, whispered.

"I don't know," a second female cook whispered. Thane heard water running and vigorous splashing and assumed the pair was washing dishes. "I don't trust Abrams's nephews. I heard Corban Abrams interfered with the roundup, and he's the reason Brida Vaughn was killed."

"No, I heard Corban was trying to protect her," the first cook replied. "I heard it from someone who was there, an eyewitness."

"No one would've died if the Strays hadn't resisted," the second cook said.

"You really believe that? You'd just let someone haul you away at gunpoint like a criminal? Are you telling me you wouldn't have fought back?"

"Thane, what are you doing?" Isaac asked.

"Are you going somewhere?" Zhao added.

Thane's eyes snapped open. He was startled to discover himself on his feet, fists clenched, moving toward the kitchen door. He turned back to the table to see Isaac and Zhao staring at him, looking confused and wary.

"Maybe it's a good thing you and *mei mei* stopped seeing each other," Zhao said. "You're crazy."

Isaac's confused expression shifted to a suspicious scowl. "You were seeing Jing?"

Thane ignored both their reactions as he returned to the table and picked up his empty plate. He glared at Zhao. "I'm not crazy." He shifted the glare to Isaac. "And it's none of your business. We need to go to work. Are you coming?"

He swallowed his anger as he took his plate to the dishwasher's alcove, forcing himself not to listen to any more of the cooks' conversation. He headed out through the double doors of the dining room, vaguely aware of two sets of footsteps behind him.

Sentry O'Rourke was still at the gates when Thane, Zhao, and Isaac walked up. She surveyed the new employees, with obvious distaste. "Where's the fourth? I was told this new team would have four members."

"Rupert will be here in a few minutes. We should probably talk to the head sentry." Thane didn't like the way O'Rourke's scowl morphed into an arrogant smirk. "Would that be you, ma'am?"

She nodded. "Right on the first guess."

Thane struggled to suppress his frustration. O'Rourke had been loyal to his uncle, blindly following his orders to imprison Nikki in the kitchen cellar, and even agreeing with Leighton's plan to banish Nikki from the fort during the night—in other words, to leave her to the night terrors, a method of execution reserved for dangerous criminals. O'Rourke also stood by and watched while Uncle attempted to strangle Corban and beat Thane senseless, only stepping in to intervene after Corban knocked Leighton out by breaking a ceramic pitcher over his head. It was clear she had no love for Strays, particularly the Abrams brothers.

This will never work. Thane suspected his former boss, Smiths Guild master Chaim Rajamani, agreed to this new assignment because he knew the tension between Thane and O'Rourke would be thick, guaranteeing the experiment would fail. *He agreed to this just to prove we should remain in exile at Fort Brida.*

To his left, Zhao and Isaac shifted uncomfortably beneath O'Rourke's gaze, but Thane refused to break eye contact. "Why don't you explain our duties to us, Ms. O'Rourke?"

O'Rourke shot him an incredulous look. She huffed a bit before stepping aside and gesturing to the open doorway behind her. "This is the sentry office."

There wasn't much to see; the tour took five minutes. The sentry area consisted of a tiny office, two holding cells, and a spiral staircase to the roof above the gates, where a narrow catwalk gave them a view of the fort's exterior. One person could manage security whether the gates were open or closed. A simple pulley system moved the massive three-story-high doors, and a set of iron bars were used to barricade the gates when they were shut.

Thane realized it didn't take much intelligence to be a sentry, which perhaps explained why O'Rourke was in charge. "What about weapons?" he asked her when they gathered outside the sentry office after the tour.

She made a sour face. "You don't need weapons to guard the gates."

"You have a weapon," Zhao pointed out.

O'Rourke gripped her wooden staff, which was the height of her shoulder. "No weapons until you've been trained to use them."

Thane snorted. "I was a hunter. I know how to use a bow and machete."

"No weapons." O'Rourke was beginning to sound like a broken recording.

"You mean to say if a night terror got inside the fort, we'd have no way of protecting people from it?" Zhao asked.

"We have gates to keep the night terrors out," O'Rourke snapped. "Now let's consider uniforms for you. I don't think—"

"But just say one found a way in," Zhao persisted.

Thane hid a smirk. He watched O'Rourke's face as she struggled to control her temper but failed.

"No night terror's ever gotten inside West Fort!"

"There's always a first time," Isaac said.

"That's enough!" O'Rourke said. "I said no weapons! Now be quiet before I sack all of you!"

"I don't think Guild Master Yarborough would be pleased to hear you didn't even give us a chance." Rupert joined the group, arms folded across his chest. He gave O'Rourke a piercing look. "And before you say,

'She'll never hear because she's in Greenfield,' I'll remind you I can send messages over any distance."

The head sentry ground her teeth, her face bright red. "Since you boys think you know everything about being sentries, you can all take the night shift—and I mean every night, from dusk till dawn."

"What about—?" Isaac sputtered.

"No uniforms, no weapons, just stand guard," O'Rourke spoke over him. "I don't care how you divide up the shift, just do it. And if a night terror *does* get in"—she turned to Zhao, with a sneer—"then we'll know who to blame." She turned on her heel, stormed back to the sentry office, and slammed the door behind her.

"That went well," Rupert said. "Off to a fun start at our new jobs."

Thane was too irritated to tell him off. "I guess we're back here in a few hours."

***

The team drew straws to see who would take the dusk to midnight shift, and Thane and Zhao pulled the short ones. Thane found his old machete stashed in the back of a dresser drawer. He tucked it under his belt and pulled on a lightweight hooded jacket. The nighttime temperatures only dropped ten degrees below the daytime temperatures on Vesta, but the nocturnal insects were a nuisance to exposed arms and faces. The jacket also offered protection from the occasional downpour.

Thane waited for Zhao in the hallway outside 30W-B, with a growing sense of trepidation. Eight years had passed since he'd been close to a night terror, and he wasn't looking forward to seeing any tonight, even from a safe vantage point on the roof. He could already hear the beasts howling in the woods outside the fort and had to turn down his hearing to steady his nerves.

Zhao hadn't spoken two words to Thane since his "not many Strays want to date Normals" remark during breakfast. Thane didn't know what to say to reassure his friend that he hadn't dumped his sister, *since that's exactly what I did.* He couldn't decide which emotion was more uncomfortable—guilt or fear.

Zhao emerged from the apartment, zipping his own hooded jacket all the way up to the week-old scruff on his chin. He yawned, gave Thane a resigned look, and fell into step with him as they headed to the gates. Neither spoke, which was fine with Thane.

A sentry Thane recognized but whose name he couldn't recall met them at the closed gates. The older man was just sliding the last iron bar into place, securing the massive doors. He turned to greet Thane and Zhao, with a curt nod. The name on his uniform said *J. Smith.*

"Good luck," Smith said before picking up his rough wooden staff and walking away.

"Goodnight," Zhao said to his retreating back.

"Let's hope it's a good night." Thane ran a tongue over his dry lips as he paused to listen to the blood-curdling growls in the forest outside the walls.

Zhao didn't appear concerned about the nocturnal racket as he led the way to the door of the sentry station. They passed the office and unoccupied holding cells before climbing the spiral staircase to the catwalk. Zhao went ahead of Thane, walking along the creaky metal span until he was at the peak of the archway, above the gates. "Be careful. I can't see a thing up here," he said over his shoulder.

"I guess that's why Isaac needed to be on the team." Thane was grateful for the iron handrails on either side of the catwalk. He didn't want to miss a step and plunge three stories to certain death—if the fall didn't kill him, the night terrors certainly would. He moved with care until he was a meter from Zhao, then turned to face the fort's exterior where a single electric spotlight illuminated a patch of ground just outside the gates.

"What are you planning to do with that machete?" Zhao asked.

Thane shrugged. "I guess I could throw it if I need to."

"I don't care what O'Rourke says—we need weapons. Look!" The word came out as a soft hiss.

Thane bit his lip and grasped the railing, with both hands, as a dozen night terrors emerged from the woods and gathered in the circle of light below him and Zhao. The beasts began pacing back and forth in front of the high doors, snarling and barking up at the sentries, their fanged muzzles dripping with saliva. It was a mystery to the colonists how the filthy predators kept their fur white.

A trickle of sweat slid down Thane's spine. His mouth was dry as he forced himself not to relive the memory of that night. His left leg gave a twinge of pain, an unwelcome reminder. *Darkness. I can't do this job.* Slaving away in a stifling smithy with Chaim breathing down his neck all day seemed like a pleasant holiday by comparison.

"I thought they avoided the light." Zhao's voice was an octave higher than normal. Thane wondered if he'd ever seen a night terror in person. "They're intelligent enough to know they can't reach us, so why do they persist?"

"Maybe they only avoid daylight," Thane said. "And maybe they're hoping we'll fall." His knuckles were turning white on the railing, so he forced himself to relax his grip. "I have no idea what we're supposed to do all night. The gates keep them out."

"We make sure no one goes outside and no night terrors get in. That's the entire job description." Zhao took a deep breath. "It's going to be a long shift."

"Yes, it is." Thane kept a firm hand on the railing as he lowered himself to a seated position on the catwalk, his legs dangling over the side.

The night terrors sent up a cacophony of fresh howls and stood on hind legs, clawing eagerly at the doors for five minutes until they seemed to realize Thane wasn't moving any closer to their hungry jaws. They returned to their pacing and snarling, never taking their beady red eyes off the two young men on the roof.

"Nasty beasts." Zhao sat next to Thane and grimaced at the night terrors' renewed enthusiasm for a potential meal. "Tomorrow night I'm bringing a bow, if I can find one. A rifle would be better."

Thane nodded. He was too busy wrestling with his own fears to say anything. He was grateful Zhao took the hint and didn't speak for the remainder of their night watch.

Over the next five hours, more night terrors joined the original pack. Some ran off in groups of threes or fours, probably to hunt for easier prey, but others emerged from the woods to take their places. By the time Rupert and Isaac came to relieve them at midnight, there were at least thirty of the predators outside the gates.

Thane's nerves were raw as he and Zhao headed back to the apartment. The thought of doing this tomorrow night, and every night for who knew how long, filled him with so much dread that he felt physically ill.

I'll have to find a way to cope, he thought. *But I have no idea how.*

TEN
INFIRMARY

Corban was feeling lonely and a little jealous that his brother and friends got to leave Fort Brida thanks to Solona's considerable influence. Now that the others had new assignments, his only visitors were Solona and Dr. DeKalb.

Surgeon Lorna DeKalb was a tiny woman, even smaller than petite nurse Solona, and at least a decade older, with dark gray hair, a deeply lined alabaster face, and a no-nonsense bedside manner. Both women treated him like a lab specimen, poking and prodding his wounds and taking his temperature several times a day. It took a few days for them to get his infection under control, although the new medical supplies and analgesic patches from the *Unity* were a big help.

"Any word on the AI?" he asked Solona on the morning of third-day, just before she scanned his forehead with a new thermometer.

"Shhhh." Solona wouldn't say anything until she scrutinized the reading, but she didn't tell him what his temperature was. "The Mechanics Guild discovered that the AI's recordings are encrypted. They've been working to break the code."

"Why would Earth send us a ship with an encrypted code?"

Solona shrugged. "Maybe they thought it might go off course and land on a hostile planet."

Corban frowned. "Since it's six storms late, that's a real possibility. The question is how did it manage to finally get here?"

"My guess is that it wasn't sent here originally. The last transmission from New Houston clearly stated that Earth was severing all ties with Vesta-Lambda due to the Plague." Solona returned the scanner to the backpack she always carried with her. She stood to leave.

"But it doesn't make sense," Corban said.

Nikki's mother studied his face, her expression thoughtful. "I can't explain it, either, but I don't consider the sudden appearance of the supply ship to be a godsend like the other colony leaders."

"What do you mean?"

"After the Plague was eradicated, I realized if we had any hope of surviving as a colony, we needed to be completely self-sufficient. We have to make do with what's here, which includes finding ways to utilize the Talents of all the Strays. Now with the forced internment and the *Unity* showing up, I feel like the colony's regressed. People would rather depend on fresh supplies than think of ways to build or invent what we need."

"I agree the timing of the *Unity* was terrible." Corban thought about the premonition and wondered how much worse things would get.

Solona nodded. "Instead of finding ways to use Talents to replace our worn-out technology, I think people will become complacent and assume more supply ships are coming."

"I see your point." Corban debated telling her about his dream, but she seemed in a hurry to leave. "Can I visit the latrine by myself and maybe get something to eat from Dagmar's station?"

Solona smiled. "Better than that, I've arranged a ride for you to Lakeside's infirmary today. We should be able to leave in an hour."

Corban couldn't help beaming at her. "Thank you, ma'am."

***

"How's my new management team working out?" Solona asked as she held the door open for Corban to step inside the apothecary.

Corban had visited the apothecary in West Fort a few times, but it was small and disorganized compared to Lakeside's. The first thing he noticed about the shelf-lined shop was the riot of competing scents. He resisted the urge to sneeze as he looked around.

The second thing he noticed was Nikki on a stepladder, arranging a shelf of glass canning jars filled with dried herbs. He sensed her confidence as she handled the inventory, and he took a minute to appreciate the view.

Nikki's thick black hair was pulled back into a ponytail, and she wore a bright yellow apron over her T-shirt and jeans. The ponytail whipped around as she turned to face the door, and she broke into one of her dimpled smiles that always made him weak in the knees. Nikki descended the ladder and rushed over to give Corban a hug.

He held her close, savoring the light that filled his mind. *I've missed you.*

Same here. He sensed that she'd found their three-day separation intolerable.

Solona cleared her throat, and they broke off the embrace, but not before Nikki captured his hand in hers as they turned to face her mother.

Corban sensed something on her mind. *Why are you upset with Solona?*

She didn't get a chance to reply before Jing emerged from a back room. "Please tell me you're staying to help. I'm dying to sit down in the dining hall for a decent meal."

Nikki snorted. "It'll be takeout, as usual." She cocked an eyebrow at Solona. "For four?"

Her mother shook her head. "Sorry, we're headed to the infirmary. I told Corban we'd stop by to see you first."

"I'm fine," he said. "I don't need to stay in the infirmary."

"You're not fine," Solona said. "Your temperature's still elevated." She crossed the store to the shelves filled with little brown bottles and selected several. "I'm going to mix up an antibiotic and anti-inflammatory, then you're going straight to the infirmary." She walked to the room Jing just exited and shut the door.

"How are you feeling?" Jing asked Corban.

He shrugged. "I thought I was doing better, but Solona doesn't seem satisfied with my progress. How're you two managing here?"

Jing frowned. "It's taken us three days to put the shop back in order after the incompetent assistant manager ran the place without supervision."

"He didn't run it at all," Nikki said. "The door was locked when we got here, and we had a flood of customers who'd waited all week for it to reopen. We struggled to assist them when nothing was put back where it was supposed to go. It's been stressful."

"Being an adult colonist is overrated." Jing smirked. "But at least we're back to civilization."

Nikki nodded. "How's Thane managing his new responsibilities?"

Jing perked up at the mention of Thane. She shot Corban a hopeful pout.

"I don't know. We didn't stop by West Fort." His voice dropped to a whisper as he shifted his eyes toward the lab door. "We didn't stop at the bridge either."

Nikki and Jing exchanged a nervous nod. "Good." Nikki followed his gaze. "We have something to share with you, something huge, but I need to talk to Mom first."

"It's huge, but you're going to keep me in suspense?" Corban arched an eyebrow at her.

"I have to, for a little while." Nikki leaned closer to kiss him but stopped short when they heard the door to the back room open. *I'll come see you every chance I get,* she thought before turning to Solona. "Jing and I need to talk to you about one of your patients, Portia Vandermeer."

A guilty expression crossed her mother's features, but then it was gone. "I'll be back as soon as I escort Corban to the infirmary."

"Bye." Corban squeezed Nikki's hand and reluctantly let go as he turned to follow Solona out of the shop.

Corban kept up with her as best he could, but he was forced to admit the fever had sapped his strength. He was grateful the walk from the apothecary to the infirmary was short. The corner suite on the first floor of the north wall bore a simple inscription on the door, *Lakeside Infirmary*, and beneath it in smaller print, *A. Hong, MD; N. Hong, PT*.

"Dr. Hong's married to Mayor Brooks's daughter, Nehal. She'll be your physical therapist," Solona told Corban as she opened the door to a small office. "After you."

A large desk covered with dilapidated books and messy piles of paper filled the small room. Seated behind the desk was a short, wiry-looking man in a gray doctor's lab coat dotted with faded pink bloodstains. He had small dark eyes like Zhao's, but his black hair had receded to the crown of his head.

"Solona, nice to see you. Is this the patient Derek warned me about?" The man got to his feet and leaned across the desk to offer Corban his hand. "Alberto Hong."

Corban managed to lean over without losing his balance. He grasped the doctor's hand. "Corban Abrams."

"Which guild?" Hong asked.

Corban winced at the traditional greeting. "I'm not sure."

Hong raised one fuzzy, black eyebrow at him. "What?"

"I've been in Hunters Guild all my life, but I can't hunt anymore. I'd like to join the herbalists, but Guild Master Kaczenski doesn't like Strays. My brother was transferred to the sentries, but I haven't heard if I can join them."

Solona spoke up from behind him. "It's complicated. Corban's in wait-and-see status right now, at least until he's fully healed."

Hong frowned at Solona over Corban's shoulder. "Wait-and-see? Did you bring his records?"

"No paper yet, although I've been told every medic will get a datapad soon. I'll have to dictate them to you from memory."

The doctor sifted through the clutter until he found a tattered sheet of paper with some blank space on it. "A datapad would be very welcomed here. Hold on, let me find a pencil." He rummaged for another minute before unearthing a pencil stub.

Solona drew a chair over for Corban and gestured to him to sit. His back gave a twinge of pain as he eased himself onto the wooden seat.

The nurse crossed her arms and leaned one hip on the edge of the desk. "Corban Abrams, age seventeen, resident of West Fort."

"Former resident," Corban interjected.

"Next of kin, Thane Abrams, older brother," Solona went on without missing a beat. "Gunshot wound to lower right side nine days ago. Bullet exited through his back, missing his liver but tearing his obliques. Surgery to repair large intestine perforation was performed by Dr. Lorna DeKalb. Twenty-eight internal sutures, nineteen external."

"I didn't know there were that many." Corban frowned up at her.

"We treated him with whatever we could get our hands on, including the last of the IVs and morphine in the colony. He was healing, but developed an infection at the exit site last fifth-day, which I've been treating with thyme compresses. With the medical supplies from the *Unity*, I've been able to give him analgesic patches at night. He's made some improvement but is still weak, as you can tell."

Corban found an interesting knot in the floorboards to stare at.

"Due to the infection, I'm recommending he be admitted to the infirmary." She placed two small brown bottles on Hong's desk. One had a white label with Corban's name and *external* written on it in feminine handwriting. The other was identical but labeled *internal.* "We're out of gelatin capsules, so he'll need two drops of the internal blend under his tongue three times a day."

"How's the taste?" Corban asked.

"Disgusting," Solona said. "Try not to vomit."

Corban grimaced. "Thanks."

"Why not take him to the hospital ship?" Hong didn't sound defensive, merely curious.

"No." Corban shook his head.

"He doesn't want to go to the hospital." Solona shrugged.

"I'm fine. I don't even need to stay here." His back disagreed, with a sudden throb of pain, but he resisted the urge to flinch.

"Because of the current political climate, I'm inclined to agree with his request not to be admitted to the hospital," Solona said.

"Why not the infirmary at his own fort?" Hong asked.

Solona snorted. "You know why. He'll be safer here, plus this is the only fort where he can receive physical therapy."

Dr. Hong finished scribbling down Solona's information. "Nehal has been eager for a new challenge. Obliques you say?" Corban didn't like the way he said "new challenge."

"Yes." Solona patted Corban on the shoulder and turned to leave the office. "I'll be back to check on him in a week."

Corban wanted to turn around to say goodbye to her, but knew that might stir up more pain. "Thank you, Solona," he said without breaking eye contact with Hong.

As soon as she shut the door behind her, Corban asked, "Are you a Stray, sir?"

Hong smirked. "Too old. My bride is a dozen storms younger than me, a fact that didn't endear me to her mother."

"Mayor Brooks." Corban nodded.

"I have the greatest respect for Strays. I think forcing them to move to Fort Brida was a huge mistake for the colony." Hong stood and came around the desk. He gripped Corban's left elbow and helped him to his feet. "Let's take a look at that gunshot wound."

"I can manage." Corban was exhausted, but he was also tired of being an invalid. He sensed the doctor's skepticism.

"If you say so. Through here." Hong guided him around the desk and opened a door to an unoccupied room with six hospital beds, three on each side, and an aisle down the middle. "Bathroom is here." Hong walked to the end of the ward and opened another door.

Corban nodded without moving beyond the office doorway. "Where do you want me?"

"Take your pick."

Easing himself into the first bed on the left, which was in front of the room's only window, Corban kicked off his boots and braced himself for more poking and prodding.

Dr. Hong removed the bandages and examined Corban's wounds without comment, rubbed some oil from Solona's *external* bottle over his stitches, and placed two drops of the *internal* bottle's contents under his tongue.

Darkness! She wasn't kidding that I'd want to vomit.

"I'll get you something to wash that down." Hong flashed him a knowing grin.

"Thanks," Corban managed between clenched teeth. He lay back on the bed and closed his eyes. He wrestled with exhaustion, like the time he woke up after the surgery to repair his intestine, although Dr. DeKalb had been kind enough to give him an injection of morphine before he was fully awake.

Too bad this isn't morphine. He swallowed the vile concoction and it burned all the way down to his belly. *Why do I want to join the Herbalists Guild?* He reflected on the fact that he originally devised this goal to impress Nikki. *Do they have to test everything on themselves before torturing other people?*

***

Nehal Hong was Corban's physical therapist. She was dark-haired, dark-skinned, attractive, petite, and not much older than Thane, but she was all business. "My Talent is touch," she explained to Corban before closing her eyes and running her soft hands over the muscles in his back and side.

Corban thought her hands were drifting too close to places he hadn't been injured, but before he could protest, she sat behind him and gripped his left shoulder, placed her right hand over the small of his back, and pressed inward, with a force he felt all the way down to his toes. Before he had a chance to gasp, she switched her hands to grasp his other shoulder and repeated the maneuver, resulting in a distinct popping sound from his lower spine.

"How's that?" Nehal asked.

"Better?" Corban assumed it was what she wanted to hear, but as he sat up straighter on the bed, he realized the tension in his back had been significantly reduced. "Darkness. It *is* better."

"The muscles on your left side are tight," Nehal said. "They've been supporting your weight since you were shot. We're going to increase the strength on your right side. I'm not going to lie; it'll be hard work. I'll be putting you through an intensive workout twice a day, starting now."

"Now?" Corban tried to think of an excuse to delay the torture session but came up blank.

"Yes, now. Stand up straight and walk the length of the room."

***

Corban tried to find a comfortable position for sleeping. He ached all over from the rigorous physical therapy session, and the nighttime patch barely took the edge off his pain. He was also exhausted from the fever and had no trouble falling asleep. Staying asleep was another matter. He woke to the sound of raised voices in the next room.

The door to Dr. Hong's office was shut, but Corban sensed the tension even though the words were muffled. Nehal and her husband disagreed over something. He caught the word *Unity* a few times, and Nehal said *no* often, but the topic of the debate eluded him.

After several minutes, the argument died down and the door opened, admitting a tunnel of light, which fell across Corban's face in the dark room. He shut his eyes reflexively. Hong walked over to his bedside and placed a large palm on Corban's forehead to check his temperature.

"I don't want to discuss this anymore, Alberto," Nehal said in a stage-whisper from the doorway. "It's crazy."

Hong muttered back. "We'll see what Kun has to say." He grasped Corban's wrist, and checked his pulse. "Now hush, or you'll wake our patient."

Despite the admonition to be quiet, Nehal continued to argue. "Kun doesn't know anything about starships—he's an herbalist. And don't tell me Chaim Rajamani knows what he's talking about either. They're insane if they think they can launch the *Unity* and return to Earth."

ELEVEN
COMPLICATIONS TIMES TWO

"You went through my patient files?" Solona rubbed her forehead and sank into her desk chair. "You had no right to do that. There's a reason I lock my desk."

"Jing picked the lock," Nikki said.

Jing opened her mouth to protest, but Nikki sent her a quelling look and continued without missing a beat. "After talking to Ms. Vandermeer, we knew we couldn't help her if we didn't know what the problem was, so I take full responsibility for breaking into your desk. We need to know what's going on. *Everyone* needs to know, Mom."

"Those files are confidential. You have to swear none of the information leaves this room."

"You *have* to tell the colony," Nikki said.

Solona emitted a weary sigh. "I'm not sure how I can be the bearer of really bad news coming on the heels of this internment."

"Tell us what you know," Jing said.

Solona stared down at her hands, which were clasped in her lap. "All the Normal girls I've examined are infertile. They have ovaries but no uteruses. In other words, they have the hormones they need to mature physically, but they can never bear children. The Zegarellium vaccine their mothers received is the only explanation. Vesta's population will shrink until no one is left."

"What about Normal boys?" Jing asked.

Solona shrugged. "I don't know. I've only examined infant sons, and their sex organs appear normal. But it won't matter if they're fertile if women can't conceive. We don't have the technology to create artificial wombs or transplant fetuses from donors—none of the organs from the *Unity* are viable." There was a catch in her voice. "None of the embryos survived the trip."

"The population won't die out if the Strays are fertile," Nikki said.

Jing sniffled and wiped her eyes with the back of her hand. "There's only a thousand Strays, and I'm sure many of them had the vaccine too. Solona's right, the population will shrink unless Earth sends more ships our way."

"I don't know why the *Unity* took so long to reach us," Solona said. "I'm sure Earth won't risk sending any more ships if they lost communication with it. Let's hope the Mechanics Guild can break the encrypted code on the AI. It's the only way we'll know what happened."

"When are you going to tell the mayors?" Nikki asked. "You said you meet with them often."

"Every day, actually." Solona sighed again. "I've been persuading them to accept Strays back into their communities."

"Like us?" Nikki asked.

"Exactly. I have enough guild masters on my side who are willing to try out Talents in various capacities. Greenfield has consented to a communication team like Thane's. I'm sending five Strays there in the morning, but it's like chipping away at a boulder with a spoon."

"You have to tell the mayors tomorrow." Nikki peered into her mother's eyes. "This can't wait. If the Strays are the only way Vesta's population survives, we can't remain in exile like second-class citizens. The Survivors need us. Using us as test subjects for certain jobs isn't enough."

"I know." Solona got to her feet. "I need to head back to Brida before dark."

Nikki thought her mother looked exhausted. "I think Eliana can manage one night without you. Let's lock the shop and go to the apartment."

Solona opened her mouth to argue but quickly shut it, her shoulders slumped in defeat. "You're right."

"It's dark already," Jing added. "I can sleep on the couch."

***

Nikki woke early, before dawn. She sat up in her bed, listening to Solona's soft snores on the other side of the room. Dressing quietly in the dark, she tiptoed past a slumbering Jing in the sitting room, found the solar flashlight in the kitchen junk drawer, and left the apartment.

The cobblestone streets were deserted this early, and it took only five minutes to reach the infirmary. The door was locked, as she expected, so she made her way to the gates and waited a few minutes until the sky turned pink. Night sentry Bjoeren gave her a wilting look before lifting the iron bars from one of the doors and pushing it open for her to step outside the fort.

"Thanks." Nikki walked north, counting windows until she came to the one closest to the corner. The fort's exterior windows were narrow, only a decimeter wide, to keep out night terrors.

Nikki paused, frowning, as she noted the white claw marks in the stone around the window frame and deeper gouges in the wood itself, as if a night terror had tried to get inside. The thought made her shudder. The creatures were vicious, but, as far as she knew, they'd never attempted to breach the fortress walls before. She made a mental note to examine other exterior windows when she had a chance.

She pressed her nose to the dirty glass and squinted, trying to make out the room, but it was too dark to see inside.

A sleepy face appeared on the other side of the pane, startling her. She clamped a hand over her mouth to muffle a shriek.

Corban raised the sash. "Nikki? What are you doing?"

"I need to talk to you."

His expression was grim. "I need to tell you something too, something I overheard last night. I'd say come on in, but I know you can't fit through the window."

"Travis couldn't fit through this window. Can you unlock the door to the office? I'll go back through the gates."

Corban nodded. "Let's hope Dr. Hong doesn't mind early-morning visitors."

"It's Nehal you have to watch out for," Nikki said. "She's scary."

"I've noticed." Corban closed the window.

Nikki returned to the gates. The one door was still ajar.

"I'll just stand here and hold the door for you, shall I?" Bjoeren came close to cracking a smile as he let her back inside the fort.

"Yes, thanks." Nikki ignored his sarcasm as she hurried to the infirmary where Corban was waiting at the door to Dr. Hong's office.

She threw her arms around him. Warmth and light flooded her mind, bypassing his dark memories for the first time. She was surprised and delighted to reach the higher level of consciousness with no effort this time. She wanted to stand there all day and soak it in.

I feel the same way, Corban thought, *but we need to talk now before the fort wakes up.*

Nikki nodded and reluctantly let him go. Corban led her back to the infirmary and sat on the only unmade bed. She sat on the bed next to his. "You first?"

Corban hesitated before blurting, "Jing's father and Chaim Rajamani plan to launch the *Unity* and return to Earth."

"That's insane!" Nikki gasped. "It'll never work!"

"That's what Nehal told her husband last night."

"Every system in the *Unity*'s offline. Have they removed the bodies from the stasis pods? They can't possibly think those can be reused! We won't even know why the *Unity* was late, not until they break the encrypted code on the AI's recordings." Nikki shook her head. "They're delusional. All the ships are one-way, designed to be stripped once they reach a colony."

"I agree, but it sounds like Kaczenski and Rajamani think there's something different about the *Unity*'s technology. They're trying to recruit people to go along with this plan. Nehal sounded upset that Dr. Hong was willing to listen."

"I wonder who else they've tried to recruit," Nikki said. "Did you hear anything else?"

"No, that's all of it. Now tell me your big news. Was it what you couldn't tell me yesterday?"

She blew out a long breath. "I had to wait until I got all the facts from Mom. She discovered that the Zegarellium vaccine had some long-term side effects."

"What kind of side effects?"

Nikki found it awkward talking to him about fertility but attempted to explain it in an emotionally detached way. "Girls born to women who had the vaccine can never have children."

Corban winced. "That would be all the Normals—every girl younger than us. What about men? Did the vaccine affect them?"

"Mom doesn't know. She's only examined Normal girls so far, but if none of them can conceive, it won't make a difference if the men are fertile."

"Did you have the vaccine?" Corban found something interesting to stare at on the floor.

"No, Mom wasn't willing to administer it to anyone immune to the Plague. By the time the vaccine was discovered, medics knew children who hadn't reached puberty were immune. Did you have it?"

Corban raised his eyes to hers. "I don't know. Maybe Thane remembers if we got it." He frowned. "If we did, I'd want to know if I'm fertile or not."

Nikki's face grew warm. "If Strays are the only colonists who can add to the population, the Survivors can't afford to exile us. Without us, the colony will die out."

"Even with us, it sounds like the colony will die out." Corban's eyes widened, and he sat up straighter. "That's it!"

"What's it?"

"The feeling I had after the landing strip premonition. I thought the explosion would be the end of the colony." He reached over and grasped her hand. "It's not the fire; it's the vaccine that will eventually wipe us out."

Because the two events weren't related, Nikki wasn't convinced of his theory, but one thing did become clear to her. "Jing's dad wants to launch the *Unity*. That might be why it explodes. We have to tell her and Zhao. Maybe they can stop him."

Corbin frowned. "They're estranged. Zhao told me his father's never listened to him."

"And Jing just moved out. She told me she'll never speak to Kun again."

"Well, someone has to convince him it's a terrible idea."

"It won't be us." Nikki grimaced. "I'm sure he remembers how we stole his truck at gunpoint."

Corban nodded. "Talk to Jing. See what she's willing to do."

"I will. And you talk to Zhao if you see him." Nikki moved to sit beside Corban and leaned over to kiss him.

Nehal Hong burst into the room before their lips met. "Excuse me? What are you doing here?"

Nikki jumped to her feet. "I was just leaving."

"How *long* were you here?" Nehal shouted after Nikki as she vacated the room.

Nikki caught a glimpse of Corban's face before she pulled the door shut. He was trying hard not to laugh. *This relationship takes a lot of effort.* She sighed and hurried back to the Zegarelli apartment.

TWELVE
ALTERED FUTURE

The dream was different. Corban was standing on the far side of the wide bridge, looking toward the landing strip, but this time he wasn't alone. Nikki was on his right, her sword at her hip. A look of anguish was on her face. Her fear mirrored his own, but Corban sensed that their apprehension wasn't about the scene they were going to witness.

Corban heard a sharp intake of breath beside him. He looked to his left and discovered Thane, his face ashen. A large amount of blood stained the front of Thane's shirt, but Corban's empathic sense told him his brother's pain was more emotional than physical.

Before he had a moment to consider why they were afraid, the *Unity* exploded. Corban threw up an arm to shield his eyes from the fireball as the force of the blast knocked him backward, off his feet. Thane and Nikki were slammed onto their backs, with grunts of shock and pain, hitting the bridge on either side of him.

"Nooooo!" Nikki screamed. She burst into tears as the smoke engulfed them, obscuring everything around them from view.

***

Corban sat up too fast, gasping from the pain in his back.

"What's wrong?" Dr. Hong threw open the door to the office. "I heard you cry out."

"It's nothing. Just a bad dream." Corban winced as he lay back down.

"Are you in pain?" Hong asked. "I could give you a new patch."

"No, I'm all right." He hoped the doctor wouldn't challenge that assertion by examining him. Corban's heart was racing so fast he thought he might have a stroke.

Hong appeared thoughtful but shrugged. "If you say so." He started to pull the door closed when Corban had a flash of inspiration.

"Wait, doc!"

Hong paused with raised eyebrows. "Yes?"

Corban plastered on an innocent expression. "I've been stuck here so long, I have no idea what's going on with the *Unity*. Did they ever break the encrypted code on the AI?"

The doctor nodded. "The mechanics are sending each fort a recorded translation today."

"How did they manage to make recordings?"

"A case of working datapads from the *Unity* is how. Mayor Brooks wants to meet with the community council tonight."

"Is there any way I could be at that meeting?" Corban asked.

Hong seemed puzzled. "I haven't even cleared you to leave the infirmary."

"I feel fine," Corban said. "Really, Solona could vouch for my fitness," he added before Hong could protest.

"I'm the doctor here—"

"Yes, sir, you are, but my temperature's been normal for two days, and your wife thinks I need to move around as much as possible. I'm ready to leave."

Hong appeared skeptical. "And where will you go if I release you?"

Corban cringed on the inside. *Darkness! I didn't think of that.* "My brother has an apartment in West Fort."

"You'll need the interim mayor's permission to enter West." Hong gave him a sympathetic frown. "Rajamani isn't as accommodating as Mayor Brooks."

That's an understatement. "How about Solona's apartment?"

Hong shook his head. "Nikki Ramirez and Jing Kaczenski live there now. Looks like you're staying here until West Fort elects a new mayor."

Corban's mouth gaped open. "How long will that take?"

Hong grinned. "Actually, they're counting the ballots right now. Cooks Guild master Gina Piroux will be mayor in a few hours, but it might take several days for her to make changes to fort policies regarding Strays."

"You already know she won, sir?"

Hong laughed. "Would *you* vote for Rajamani if you were old enough to vote?"

"That's one of those 'does a trashbird eat trash' kinds of questions." Corban grinned.

"Patience, my young patient, you'll soon be free," Hong said. "Oh, and you have a visitor in my office."

Corban sat up again. "Why didn't you tell me?"

The doctor stepped out of the room, and Thane walked in. "How're you feeling?"

Corban feigned disappointment. "I was hoping you were Nikki."

"Nice." Thane limped over to the bed and dropped a duffle bag on Corban's feet. "I even had these laundered for you. I won't make that mistake again."

"Kidding." Corban grimaced. "I'm kidding. Thanks for the clothes." He pulled the bag toward him and unzipped it. "Finally I can put on clean underwear after I shower."

Thane rolled his eyes. "My nose thanks you. I can't stay long."

Corban noted the dark circles beneath his brother's eyes. "You look tired."

"O'Rourke gave us the night shift," Thane said. "It takes some getting used to."

"Darkness."

"Yes, we get plenty of that. I guess it makes for less tension since no one knows a bunch of Strays are on sentry duty every night."

"But you're supposed to be a communication team?" Corban asked. "You send messages to the other forts?"

"So far the only message Rupert's sent is how many night terrors are outside the gates, and that number is huge. I didn't know there were so many, and they claw at the doors like they're starving. Now I know how you felt sitting up in that tree."

"No, you don't know how I felt since you were safe inside the fortress walls and I was hanging onto a branch all night, praying they couldn't climb up and get me." Corban frowned, but couldn't muster the energy to worry about the night terror population. "West Fort could do so much more with your Talents."

Thane shrugged, his expression troubled. "We're lucky they let us in the fort at all."

"It's not fair they treat us like second-class citizens."

"Nothing about colony life is fair, but being back in West gives me one advantage."

"What's that?" Corban asked.

"Access to information. I found out the mayors are meeting with Solona this afternoon, in Chaim's apartment."

"They're going to listen to the AI's recording before meeting with their community councils tonight?"

"I think so," Thane said.

"Do you have someone to take notes?"

Thane shrugged and sat on the bed next to Corban's. "Rhubarb's handwriting is illegible, so that leaves Zhao or Isaac, and since Isaac doesn't like me, that leaves Zhao, or it would if Zhao wasn't mad at me too."

"What? What's Isaac's problem? And I thought you got along fine with Zhao."

"Isaac heard I was seeing Jing. I guess he likes her." Thane scowled. "Zhao isn't happy I stopped seeing Jing, even though he's the one who warned me to leave her alone."

"No, Zhao told you to stop giving her mixed messages. He didn't tell you to dump her."

Thane's face reddened. "I didn't dump her."

Corban arched an eyebrow at him. "Whatever you want to call it. So you need a scribe for this afternoon?"

"And tonight. I'm interested to hear what the community council does with this new information."

"I can't get past Warden Hong for a few more days, so I can't help you. You could ask Nikki."

"The second meeting's at night," Thane said. "I don't know where she could stay in West."

"Ms. Vaughn?" Their former science teacher Emily Vaughn had come to their aid before. Brida Vaughn, the young woman their uncle Leighton murdered, had been her adopted daughter.

Thane nodded. "Good idea. I'll ask her."

"Nikki's at the apothecary in the marketplace if you want to talk to her."

"Doesn't Jing work there too?" Thane's brow furrowed.

Corban folded his arms. "You can't avoid her forever."

Thane sighed and got to his feet. "I know."

"Wait, before you go, do you remember if we had the Zegarellium vaccine?"

"We didn't. Why?" Thane asked.

"Solona discovered some side effects."

"What kind of side effects?"

"Infertility in Normal girls whose mothers had the vaccine."

Thane gaped at him. "What about males? Any side effects passed down from fathers to sons?"

"She doesn't know yet."

"Darkness. This is why Solona was upset that none of the embryos on the *Unity* survived."

Corban nodded. "There's two more things I need to tell you." He glanced toward the office door to make sure it was still shut before lowering his voice to a whisper. "Kun and Chaim are planning to launch the *Unity* and return to Earth."

"What? That's impossible!" Thane's reaction mirrored Nikki's earlier.

"Shhhh. Keep your voice down. I don't know how they think they'll accomplish this, but they've been working to recruit others, like Dr. Hong. I think this is what I saw in my premonition. This launch attempt is why the *Unity* explodes."

Thane's brow furrowed. "You may be right about that. We've got to let people know about your premonition."

"I agree. Maybe you could convince Jing to talk to her father."

Thane grimaced. "Sounds like a job for Nikki."

"I think Jing would be willing to do it for you."

Thane snorted. "Maybe last week she would've. Today she'll probably refuse to listen to anything I say."

"You have to try," Corban said. "People are going to die if they attempt this. It's suicide."

"I'll do what I can. You said you had two things to tell me."

Corban nodded. "I had the premonition again, about the *Unity* exploding."

Thane's brow furrowed. "Something changed?"

"Yes, this time I wasn't alone. You and Nikki were with me. All three of us were on the bridge when it blew."

"We were all there. But why?"

"I don't know, but Nikki started screaming and crying." He studied Thane's face for a reaction. "What do you think it means?"

Thane's frowned deepened. "Nikki's reaction sounds like grief."

Corban experienced a tremor of fear. "Someone was on the *Unity*?" He hated to give voice to the thought. "Maybe Solona?"

"We have to convince Kun and Chaim to abandon this plan." Thane gnawed his lower lip. "I'll talk to Zhao, and I'll work on getting you assigned to the West Fort sentries when you're well enough to leave."

"Thanks, and thanks for coming to see me." Corban didn't have the heart to tell Thane he'd prefer to stay in Lakeside with Nikki.

THIRTEEN
THANE'S WALL

Thane took his time walking toward the apothecary. He'd never been to Lakeside before so he explored the busy marketplace with interest. Unlike West Fort, which was still functioning under a cloud of tension in the aftermath of the Stray roundup, Lakeside seemed to be a cheerful and carefree place. People were going about their business, bartering with vendors for wares and services.

Conditions normal. He peered into the smithy where one Survivor was pounding away at something the size of a truck hood on his anvil.

"What are you making?" Thane shouted to be heard over the clang of the metal-smith's hammer. He stepped inside the shed, noting there was only one forge. The coals in the brazier glowed orange, heating the small workspace to an uncomfortable temperature. Thane didn't miss working in a stifling smithy under the supervision of Chaim Rajamani.

The metal-smith stepped away from his work. His face was hidden behind a welding mask but Thane thought he seemed familiar. "Chaim wants me to smooth the edges of the airlock door for the *Unity*."

Thane was startled. "Why?"

"No idea." The smith raised his mask, revealing a lined face streaked with sweat, and an auburn mustache streaked with gray. "He thinks we should put the ship back together instead of stripping it down this time."

"You're Rupert's uncle, aren't you?" Thane asked. "You look just like him."

The smith squinted at him before nodding. "Bertram Conquist. Rupert's dad was my twin brother. You're Thane Abrams?"

Thane offered his hand. "Twin brother?"

"Identical twins. That's why Rupert looks like me." Conquist's palm was thick with calluses and damp with perspiration, but he shook Thane's hand and broke into a lopsided grin exactly like his nephew's. "My brother Bernard died in the Plague, but you probably know that. How's Rupert? I haven't seen him for several storms."

"He's doing well. He's a sentry now."

"Sounds like a better use of his Talent than being bullied by Chaim Rajamani," Conquist said. "This job's become unbearable since that trashbird was made guild master."

Thane silently agreed. "So you're not one of the Survivors who helped banish the Strays to Fort Brida?"

Conquist shook his head. "It took me some time to get used to the idea of having a Stray for a nephew, but after the violence of the internment, I realized whose side I needed to be on. I never imagined Survivors would force the Strays out at gunpoint." His face fell.

"I only wish I'd told Rupert I accepted his Talent a long time ago. I've missed him."

"I'm sure he'd be happy to see you again, sir." Thane had no idea if Rupert would be pleased to see his uncle, but Conquist's remorse appeared genuine. "We live in apartment 30W and work the night shift, so come over anytime during the day."

"I will." The metal-smith gripped Thane's hand again. "It's good to meet you in person. Sorry to hear about your uncle Leighton."

Thane couldn't hold back a snort of derision. "Don't be. It's wonderful to be free of him."

Conquist didn't appear surprised at this confession. "Tell Rupert hello and that I'll come to visit him soon."

"I will, sir. Goodbye." Thane stepped outside the stifling shed. He was heartened to think there were probably more Survivors like Bertram Conquist who opposed the internment and wanted the Strays restored to their homes and guilds. He tried to savor the optimism as he approached the apothecary.

Here goes nothing. A little bell chimed as he opened the glass door into the neat shop. Nikki glanced up from behind a long counter where she was helping an old woman choose from an assortment of tiny brown bottles.

"I'll be with you in a moment, sir."

Sir? Thane was taken aback by her cool tone and stern expression, but he nodded politely and scanned the shop for Jing. Two doors were at the back, and both were closed. He shoved his hands into the hip pockets of his jeans and waited, trying not to fidget.

The customer Nikki was assisting exited the shop a few minutes later, carrying a single bottle. There were no other customers in the apothecary.

"How're you managing your new responsibilities?" Nikki asked without preamble, her tone a trifle warmer, although she showed no inclination to approach him.

"Not so well," Thane said. "We're stuck with the night shift because our supervisor is O'Rourke."

Nikki's eyes widened. "The slime worm who stuck me in the cellar and left me there, tied up?"

"The same. She's as charming as ever."

"Did you come to Lakeside to see Corban?"

Thane tried not to show irritation at the abrupt topic shift. "Yes, and to ask for your help."

Nikki squinted at him. "My help?"

"Yes, the mayors and your mother are meeting this afternoon in West Fort, and I need a scribe."

Nikki focused on his face, her expression wary.

"They have the translated AI report. They're going to discuss it before they meet with their respective forts tonight. If you're willing, I'd like you to also write down what I overhear at the night meeting."

"I can't stay—" she began.

"I'll ask Ms. Vaughn if you could stay with her," Thane said.

Nikki bit her lip. "You think they're going to discuss this insane plan to launch the *Unity*?"

"Corban just told me about that, and yes, I do."

"Count me in." Nikki came around the counter and gestured for him to follow her to one of the doors at the back of the shop. "I'm not happy with the way you treated Jing, but I know I need to get over it since you're Corban's brother."

Thane tried to get a word in but Nikki spoke over him. "Let's see if Jing's willing to run the apothecary solo for the rest of the day. You should be the one to ask her."

He couldn't think of a valid reason to object. He paused a few meters from the right-hand room and watched with trepidation as Nikki opened the door. He glimpsed a large work-table overflowing with piles of roots and leaves. The potent scent of rosemary filtered into the shop.

"Jing, someone to see you."

Not the words Thane would have chosen, but he squared his shoulders and tried to conjure a neutral expression on his face.

Jing came to the door and frowned at Thane. She was wearing a bright yellow apron covered with green stains over torn jeans and a purple T-shirt, her black hair pulled up into a messy bun. He'd always thought Jing was attractive but managed to convince himself she was too young for him. She was prone to emotional outbursts and plenty of tears but could be tough and tenacious when she needed to be. His heart rate sped up as he was forced to admit to himself that he'd missed her.

"Hello, Jing."

"*Hello?* You didn't even say *goodbye.*" Her tone was ice cold.

Thane knew he deserved this response. "I'm sorry."

"*Sorry* doesn't make up for what you did." Jing marched over to him until they were toe to toe. She stared into his face, her expression furious. "You dumped me."

"I didn't mean to—"

"So you're saying you didn't plan to let me leave without saying goodbye?" Jing sneered. "And you think *I'm* the immature one?"

"I never said—" Thane sputtered.

"You didn't need to! You didn't have the courage to say anything to me! All you had to say was 'we shouldn't see each other anymore,' but you thought it was easier to hide—you coward!'"

"I said I'm sorry." Thane reined in his desire to retaliate, to shout at her about her suffocating neediness and unreasonable expectations. He felt helpless, as if he were enduring a verbal lashing from his abusive uncle. "I didn't mean to hurt you."

"Well, you did!" Tears glistened in her eyes.

"I'm wrong for you." The words were out of his mouth before he could stop them.

Jing froze, her expression a mix of confusion, anger, and shock.

Thane went on before he lost his nerve. "I told you before you deserve someone who's whole."

"I can't believe you measure your worth by that." Jing pointed at his brace. "Or maybe you just use it as a convenient excuse?"

He almost recoiled from the venom in her words but knew he deserved them because they were accurate. "When you put it that way, I guess I am a coward." He took a step back, steeling his nerve to walk away, although he was certain it would be a mistake he'd regret for the rest of his life.

Her expression softened as she studied his face. "No, no, I'm sorry I called you a coward. You're the bravest person I've ever known, next to Nikki." She took a deep breath. "I think you need to know I'm wrong for you too."

"Jing!" Nikki's hiss was sharp. "Don't!" Thane had forgotten she was still in the shop, witnessing this painful scene, a scene he'd tried so hard to avoid.

"I had the vaccine." Tears slid down Jing's face. "Any children I have will be infertile. You need someone who can help the colony survive. You need to marry a Stray."

Marriage was the furthest thing from Thane's mind, but he recognized that what Jing was saying was important to her. He was torn between the desire to take her in his arms and comfort her or walk away so she wouldn't get her hopes up again. He watched her cry, wishing he knew what to say, ashamed at his inability to make things right between them.

"I don't care that you had the vaccine," he whispered.

"And I don't care that you have a bad leg!"

"I just came here to ask"—he started to say Nikki, but something stopped him—"I came to ask *you* to be a scribe for me. I need to eavesdrop on the mayors meeting at West Fort and—"

He didn't get a chance to finish because Jing launched herself at him. She seized his shoulders, pulled his face down to hers, and kissed him. Her face was slippery with tears, but she seemed determined to give him mouth-to-mouth resuscitation.

"You two would probably like to be alone." Thane heard Nikki clear her throat, but didn't take time to process her words as he focused on kissing Jing, his entire body coursing with emotions he'd been trying to suppress for weeks. He marveled at how incredible she felt in his arms, how all his doubts seemed to melt away the instant their lips met.

"I want you in my life," Thane whispered when he came up for air. "I'm sorry I've been an idiot."

"Apology accepted." Jing flashed a mischievous grin. "How was that for a first kiss?"

"First kiss?" Nikki burst into laughter. "Really? This was the first time you two kissed?"

Thane was annoyed Nikki hadn't given them any privacy, as she'd suggested. He raised his chin to glance over at her, but kept his arms wrapped around Jing.

"You're one to talk." Jing chuckled. "You ran straight at Corban, chopped off his uncle's head, then— "

"Did just what you did with Thane," Nikki interrupted, "tears and all. I was hysterical."

Thane's mind was spinning from the emotional overload. He stroked Jing's shoulders, aware that this was the first time he'd let down his guard and allowed someone to get close to him. He'd spent so much of his life actively trying to avoid physical and emotional pain that he didn't realize how impenetrable his wall had become, not until Jing came along.

He'd been attracted to her from the moment they met. Trying to avoid her made him miserable. He was nervous at the thought of causing her more pain if their relationship didn't work out, but he knew he couldn't use his injury as an excuse anymore.

"You deserve to be happy after living with a monster for sixteen years." Nikki gave him a measured look before facing Jing. "You both deserve to be happy."

Thane struggled to get his thoughts in order. "Nikki, would you mind running the shop by yourself for the rest of the day? Jing and I need to find a ride to West Fort."

"I'd be happy to." Nikki adjusted her apron and headed back toward the long counter. "Say hello to Ms. Vaughn for me."

***

A bored-looking Farmers Guild truck driver let Thane and Jing hitch a ride. "I'm headed to Waterfall but I'll let you off at the fork in the road. West's only a kilometer from there."

"That'll be fine, thanks. We appreciate it." Thane took a seat on the open tailgate next to Jing. They dangled their legs over the road and sat with their arms wrapped around each other's waist.

Thane was content to sit in silence, but Jing had a lot on her mind. He half-listened to her describe the past week in vivid detail. When she mentioned the *Unity*, he knew the time had come to speak up. "Nikki told you what Corban overheard?"

"About my father and Rajamani wanting to launch the ship and return to Earth?" Jing scoffed. "Impossible. They're delusional."

"But what if they're not? What if they figure out a way? Today I talked to a metal-smith who was working on the airlock door, repairing it."

"The ships are designed to travel one way." Jing shook her head. "I'm not worried."

The truck turned south, passing the wide bridge that led to the landing strip. A knot of fear formed in Thane's stomach. "Corban's premonition about the *Unity* exploding—what if it happens because your dad tries to launch it?"

"It's impossible!" Jing sounded uncertain.

"What if they succeed? He'd die when the *Unity* blows up. So would everyone on board. Corban saw it happen. His premonitions are never wrong."

"It's so far-fetched." Jing gripped his hand tighter. "*Baba*'s smart. He'll realize it won't work."

"People do irrational things when they're obsessed with an idea. Look at how much damage Uncle did when he convinced people to segregate the Strays. You have to talk to your dad and warn him."

Jing was quiet for a few minutes.

"He'll listen to you," Thane said.

"As long as we keep Corban away from the bridge, it won't happen." Jing sounded as if she was trying to convince herself.

"We can't ignore this and hope it never happens. People will die if we don't warn them. Corban had the premonition again, last night."

"Did he see something different this time?"

"Yes, he saw me and Nikki. We were with him on the bridge. Corban said Nikki was terrified. She screamed and started sobbing when the ship blew up."

Jing turned her head to look at him, her mouth pinched into a thin line. "Why would she do that?"

"We think someone was on the *Unity* when it blew. Maybe Solona, we don't know. Someone important to her." A thought hit him hard: *Maybe it was someone important to me too.* Thane didn't dare admit what he was thinking. It was too horrible to imagine.

"Darkness." Jing leaned against him, and he instinctively drew her closer. "How's your rib?"

"Better." Thane dismissed her attempt to change the subject. "Do you see why you have to talk to your father? You're the only one he'll listen to."

"Zhao?" she said, uncertainty in her tone.

"Has he ever listened to Zhao?"

"No." Jing sniffled. "You're right. I'll try to reason with him."

Thane gave her a reassuring squeeze. "I'd be glad to help you with that conversation, but I don't think your father would be pleased to find out you're seeing a Stray."

Jing chuckled. "He threatened to cut off Isaac's, um, manhood, if he took me to the guild formal."

Thane burst into laughter. "So that's why Isaac doesn't like me. Good to know. I'll be sure to forge a suit of armor before asking your dad"—the words were out of his mouth before he had a chance to re-consider—"for your hand."

He'd said it in jest, but Jing's eyes widened. "You'd do that?"

"Maybe. Someday." Thane's face turned crimson as he stared down at the road. *Why don't my filters work around her? I can't believe I said that.* "Maybe, when you're older . . ." his voice trailed off. He knew how pathetic it sounded.

Jing tilted her head back and gazed into his eyes, but all he could focus on were her full lips, which were curled into a hopeful smile. He leaned down and kissed her, gently at first, but Jing responded with a passion that took his breath away.

Thane was surprised when the truck stopped and the driver banged on the back window for them to get off. He'd lost all track of time.

"Thank you, sir!" Jing's face was pink as she took Thane's hand and they started down the road toward West Fort.

"Sorry I'm slow," Thane said.

"Don't apologize for your leg." Jing turned to him, with eyes blazing. "Not to me. Not ever."

Thane's lips flapped a few times before he managed a flabbergasted, "Yes, ma'am."

"Your brace is a badge of honor. You almost lost your life rescuing your brother, and I don't ever want to hear a disparaging word about it again. Got it?"

Thane nodded.

"Good, now that we're clear on that, let's discuss what to tell Zhao about us." Jing's snarl morphed into a mischievous grin.

Thane just laughed. *What have I gotten myself into?*

***

"Who's this?" O'Rourke held out her staff, blocking Jing's entry at the gateway to West Fort.

Thane was tempted to snatch the staff from his boss's hands and break it over her head. "This is Jing Kaczenski. She's *Normal.* Her father's Herbalists Guild master, Kun Kaczenski."

"Any relation to Zhao?" O'Rourke's suspicious scowl didn't waver.

"My brother." Jing gripped Thane's hand tighter. "Now please let us by."

"No one enters without my permission." O'Rourke took a threatening step toward Jing.

Thane moved to block the sentry. He didn't want to lose his job, but he wasn't going to take any more harassment from his unpleasant supervisor. "I'm a resident of West Fort, and I'm allowed to have guests."

"You shouldn't even be here!" O'Rourke rounded on him, the color rising in her cheeks. "I told Chaim it would be a mistake to let Strays back in!"

"Then it's a good thing it's not his decision to make," interrupted a cold voice behind O'Rourke. Gina Piroux approached the sentry, hands on her hips. Thane almost expected her to whip out a meat cleaver as she did during the roundup.

O'Rourke took a step back from Thane and stood at attention. "Madam Mayor, I was just telling—"

"I heard what you were 'just telling' Mr. Abrams and Ms. Kaczenski. The whole fort could hear you. Your prejudice attitude is no longer welcome here."

"Ma'am?" O'Rourke appeared nervous.

"Yes, you heard me. As of today, West Fort is a Stray sanctuary, like Lakeside."

"But"—the sentry tried to get a word in—"you can't—"

"Oh, I can. The community council just voted to approve it. Oh, and you're fired."

O'Rourke's face fell. "But, ma'am—"

Mayor Piroux put a finger to her lips and gestured for the sentry to walk away. "You might want to let Guild Master Yarborough know you need to find another post, although I understand she's been getting daily reports from Mr. Conquist. She might not want to keep you in the guild."

Thane almost felt sorry for the sentry. Almost. O'Rourke let her staff drop to the ground before turning around and walking into the fort, without another word, although from her clenched jaw, he suspected she had many things she'd like to say if she had the chance.

"Thank you, ma'am." He smiled at Mayor Piroux. "And congratulations on winning the election."

She chuckled but fixed both of them with her steely gaze. "There's going to be an important meeting at Rajamani's in a few minutes, but the gates always need a sentry. Maybe you'd like to take over for O'Rourke until one of your friends can relieve you? I understand the sentry's office is fairly soundproof with the door closed." The new mayor winked at him before turning around and heading back into West Fort.

"I like her," Jing managed after a stunned silence. She picked up O'Rourke's abandoned staff. "And this might come in handy."

"Stray sanctuary?" Thane laughed. "Chaim's going to have a purple crawler."

"I think he'll have a whole litter!"

Thane stepped over to the sentry office door and tried the knob. It was unlocked. He drew Jing inside and shut the door behind them. A quick peek down the short hallway to the holding cells confirmed they were both empty. A small window in the upper half of the door gave him a view of the archway between the open gates, but he wasn't expecting any trouble. *People should be free to come and go from any fort.*

"Look at this!" he said. There was a datapad on the desktop. "Looks like someone got supplies from the *Unity*."

Jing leaned the staff against the wall and scanned the tiny office. "Where can I sit?"

Thane dropped into the only chair and backed her onto his lap. He snaked both arms around her waist and buried his face in her jasmine-scented hair. "This works for me."

"I think you'll be a bit distracted." Jing loosened his grip and shifted forward so she was perched on his right knee. She slid the datapad in front of her on the desk and opened a blank page. "You need to listen closely."

"No problem. I can concentrate better with you here," Thane said.

"What? You just made that up." Jing laughed.

"No, it's true. If I don't have to wonder where you are, what you're doing, if you're safe, if you spend as much time thinking about me as I do about you—"

"Shhh," Jing interrupted his rambling. "I get it. I'm here so you're not daydreaming about me. Now focus, we have a job to do."

"Yes, ma'am." Thane shut his eyes and scanned the audio babble inside the walls of the fort, picking through dozens of conversations for a familiar voice. He was able to hone in on Solona Zegarelli's and knew the meeting had begun.

FOURTEEN
THE AI'S REPORT

"Look what I've got!" Jing appeared in the doorway of the apothecary compounding lab.

Nikki stepped away from the pulpy pink mass of crushed rose hips in the base of the stone mortar. She set the pestle down. "What?"

Jing waved a datapad at her.

"Where did you get that?" Nikki came around the table.

"Stole it from West's sentries' office—with Mayor Piroux's approval. Oh, and she said we can keep this to track inventory here at the shop."

"And Mom can get her patient files properly recorded." Nikki grinned. "No more scraps of paper and old index cards."

"Piroux even got her hands on a datapad for Fort Brida. The Stray census will be on a real spreadsheet."

"That's great! Derek's job just got easier, which should make Eliana happy."

Jing logged on and opened a document. "Here are the transcripts from both meetings yesterday. And wait till you hear this: West is now a Stray sanctuary! Ms.

Vaughn threw an impromptu party last night when Thane and I told her. I think half the fort was in her apartment." She yawned, for emphasis.

"It's a good thing Ms. Piroux was elected. Maybe all the Strays can get their lives back with two mayors on our side."

"Three mayors," Jing said. "Mayor Jesperson of Orchard Valley wants the Strays back too. You'll read what she said in the transcript. I think your dad had steam coming out his ears when she announced it."

"My father was there?" Nikki took the wafer-thin tablet from Jing.

"Yes, he's spearheading the plan to launch the *Unity*. Thane said he's never heard a group of adults scream at each other like they did at that meeting, at least not without throwing punches."

"I'm sure Mom loved having the trashbird in attendance. How about the community council meeting?"

"Much quieter, but still lots of arguing. The Survivors are definitely split over what to do with the *Unity*."

"Perfect name for the ship." Nikki rolled her eyes. She turned the datapad over in her hands to examine it. "I've never seen a device that didn't need recharging. The technology has definitely advanced in sixteen storms."

"Never mind that"—Jing tapped the screen impatiently—"read it."

The bell on the apothecary door tinkled before Nikki skimmed the first line.

"I've got it." Jing hurried back into the main shop.

Nikki leaned her elbows on the work table and read Jing's transcript.

Mayors Meeting

Chaim Rajamani: Since this is my home, I'll conduct. I think we all know each other, but let's go around and introduce ourselves for the official record.

(In attendance) Chaim Rajamani (Smiths GM), Solona Zegarelli, Kun Kaczenski (Herbalists GM), Mayor Gina Piroux (West Fort, Cooks GM), Mayor Pavitra Brooks (Lakeside), Mayor Mariposa Savoy (East Fort), Mayor Jonah DeKalb (Waterfall), Mayor Derek Graham (Brida), Elian Ramirez (Farmers GM), Dr. Alberto Hong, Dr. Lorna DeKalb (Medics GM), Mayor Afshan Qualls (Greenfield, Textiles GM), Mayor Faith Ann Jesperson (Orchard Valley).

Nikki was relieved not every guild master was in attendance, otherwise the roll, and the meeting itself, would've been much longer. With her father sitting in and Jing's mention of screaming, she already knew the drama level would be high.

Rajamani: First order of business is the translation of the *Unity*'s AI report. I've asked Mayor DeKalb to share that with us.

JDeKalb: Since there are one hundred and seventy-eight hours of recordings, I asked the Mechanics Guild technicians to give us a summary. Most of the entries are about ship's maintenance, so I'm sure you don't want to hear "checked fuel rods" and "checked stasis pods" fifteen hundred times.

Ramirez: Get to the point. Why the delay? Did the ship go off course?

Yes, leave it to my father to open his big mouth, Nikki thought.

JDeKalb: I'm getting to that, Elian. So here's what happened. The *Unity* was bound for Vesta-Gamma, not Vesta-Lambda.
Ramirez: What? How?
JDeKalb: I'm getting to that.
Zegarelli: Yes, Elian, hush, and let the man speak.
Ramirez: I don't take orders from—
Piroux: Be quiet! This is my fort, and I give the orders here! Shut your mouth or get out, Ramirez!

That didn't take long. Nikki scrolled past the bickering until she found DeKalb's name again.

JDeKalb: Approximately four storms into the four and a half storm voyage, the *Unity* was struck by a large asteroid and knocked off course.
Graham: That doesn't sound severe enough to send it our way.
JDeKalb: The asteroid struck the bridge.
Graham (and others): Oh.
JDeKalb: The power went out, and the ship tumbled (pause) for almost two storms. (Thane's comment: assorted gasps and muttering.) It took the AI that much time to repair the engines. At that point the *Unity* was twenty light-years off course and much closer to Lambda than Gamma. The AI was programmed to bring the ship down safely in the event of an emergency, supposedly to preserve the lives of the colonists in stasis. With the power out that long, there wasn't a chance of anyone surviving. (Pause) The AI recalculated the navigation coordinates and

set the autopilot to land the *Unity* here. As far as I know, Earth has no idea where the ship is. The power was restored, but most systems remained offline, including communication.

Rajamani: Thank you, Mayor DeKalb. Now I'd like to move on to our next topic. I'm sure you've all heard the rumors, but I want to explore an idea that Kaczenski, DeKalb, and I have been considering. Can we use the *Unity* as more than a supply ship?

Kaczenski: In other words, can we use it to return to Earth?

(Thane: five minutes of arguing, too many voices to single out individual opinions.)

Rajamani: Let me finish, please!

Zegarelli: You're insane. The bridge took a direct hit from an asteroid. Even if you could launch the ship, what makes you think it's stable enough to return to Earth?

Ramirez: Let the man speak, Stray lover!

Rajamani: Order! Be quiet, Elian, or I'll let Piroux kick you out!

Piroux: I'd be happy to.

Ramirez: (Censored.)

Rajamani: (Speaking over Ramirez) As I was saying, Kaczenski, DeKalb, and I studied the ship's technology and have come to the conclusion that the fuel rods are reusable . . . as are the stasis pods.

(Lots of shocked muttering.)

Rajamani: When we moved the bodies to the Shrine last week—thank you, Dr. Hong, for the use of the hazmat suits—once the pods were emptied, we took a closer look at them. They can be powered up and programmed for another voyage.

JDeKalb: It's true. They can be reused indefinitely, just like the fuel rods. The *Unity* has a more advanced technology than we've ever seen. Just look at the datapads—they never need recharging.

Piroux: So the technology is more advanced, but let's consider why this might be a bad idea. For one thing, why do we want to attempt to go back to Earth? Our ancestors came here to escape Earth. Vesta-Lambda is a successful colony.

Ramirez: It was before the Strays.

Zegarelli: Shut your mouth! You and your buddy Leighton Abrams are the reason the colony's divided! You've practically imprisoned one-tenth of our population! Young people who are vital to the colony's survival!

(Another five minutes of heated arguing.)

Rajamani: Order, please! Mayor Piroux brought up a valid point, so if we could discuss this like civilized people? Why would anyone want to go back to Earth?

(Long pause, muttering.)

JDeKalb: How about just to let them know we survived the Plague, and that we deserve their support again?

Piroux: Couldn't we accomplish the same thing with a transmission?

JDeKalb: Our satellite has been offline for ten storms, and there's no guarantee we can get the *Unity*'s transmitter working again.

(General debate for several minutes.)

Zegarelli: I have something I need to say. It has to do with Vesta's survival. (Pause.) I've examined dozens of Normal girls, and I've discovered the ones born to Survivor mothers who had the Zegarelli vaccine (long pause) are infertile.

Piroux: What are you saying?

Zegarelli: I'm saying our population is going to shrink to unsustainable numbers because Normals can't conceive.

LDeKalb: Why haven't you shared this information with the Medics Guild, Solona?

Zegarelli: I'm sorry I put it off. I was hoping I was wrong, but in every case, the results have been the same. Normal girls born to Survivor women who had the vaccine . . . do not have uteruses.

(Lots of muttering.)

Zegarelli: Strays will be the only ones who can add to the population, and even that will be limited to female Strays who didn't have the vaccine. I know some parents wanted their daughters to have the vaccine, just in case. It was a huge mistake, one we could never have foreseen.

Ramirez: Sounds like an excellent reason to leave!

(Thane: Ten minutes of heated arguing until Mayor Jesperson manages to be heard above the shouting.)

Jesperson: There are only twenty stasis pods, Chaim. Since you seem determined to attempt this, who do you plan to take with you?

Ramirez: No Strays, that's obvious!

Jesperson: Why not?

Ramirez: Because they don't belong on Earth. They're native to Vesta, the whole worthless bunch of them.

Zegarelli: Yes, please leave! Take the ship and get the (censored) off this planet! Let's get twenty narrow-minded slime worms (censored) off this colony! We'll all be better off without you!

Jesperson: (Speaking over Solona) Which reminds me—Orchard Valley community council voted last night to allow Strays back into our fort. The internment never set well with me, so this is just a small step to rectify an unacceptable situation.

(Smattering of applause)

Piroux: Well done, Faith Ann!

Ramirez: (Censored)

(Another five minutes of shouting.)

Piroux: I think we need to adjourn this meeting until some of you can start behaving like adults. Chaim, your team can tinker with the *Unity* all you want, but you need to keep the mayors informed of your plan to launch, if you figure out how to make it happen. Do the other mayors concur?

(Mumbled assents.)

Graham: I don't, but maybe if Chaim and company are preoccupied, the Strays can get back to the business of living our lives without harassment.

Jesperson: Well said!

Piroux: I just fired my head sentry for bullying my new communication team. You wouldn't know anything about that would you, Chaim?

Ramirez: You're all a bunch of (censored).

Piroux: This meeting's over! And you will *not* be invited to the next one, Ramirez! Get out!

(More arguing, name calling, and veiled threats. People leave the apartment.)

Nikki sighed. *That was ugly. I feel bad Thane had to listen to all of it.* She scrolled down to the next transcript.

West Fort Community Council Meeting

In attendance: Mayor Gina Piroux and six council members, including Emily Vaughn.

Nikki didn't recognize the names of the other five council members.

Piroux: This is what we know about the *Unity* from the AI's recordings.

The same information from the mayors meeting was shared, but the community council handled the news without the verbal sparring. They discussed the pros and cons of launching the *Unity*, along with the long-term implications of the Normals' infertility.

Vaughn: I propose that we welcome the Strays back as soon as possible. Let them return to their homes and jobs. We need to restore good relations if we're dependent on them for the colony's survival.

Piroux: How do we handle the colonists who supported the internment? I fired my head sentry for harassing a Normal, just because she was with a Stray. There are plenty more like her.

Vaughn: I'm not sure how to handle the tension. It was there before the roundup, and it will continue even when the Strays come home, although I'm sure many of them will choose to stay at Fort Brida after everything that's happened.

Piroux: My daughter, for one. Dagmar told me she doesn't mind living under primitive conditions if she can avoid the daily harassment from Survivors. How will I have grandchildren if no Survivor will give her a second look?

Vaughn: And the colony needs her to have children, as many as possible.

Piroux: Don't tell her that. She's already under enough pressure from me. (Laughter.) All right, this is the plan: Chaim and his team are going to work on the *Unity* to see if it's possible to make a return trip. The rest of us are going to reach out to the Strays and welcome them back to West. I'm heading over to Brida tomorrow morning. Anyone want to go with me?

Vaughn: I do.

(A few other positive responses.)

Jing poked her head in the doorway. "What do you think?"

"I think we need to share Corban's premonition with the colony leaders, at least the ones who'll listen to us. Just the idea of being near the ship makes me nervous. Tinkering with the engines sounds suicidal."

"Thane said people aren't rational when they're obsessed with an idea. That describes *Baba* perfectly."

"I don't understand what your dad expects to work on." Nikki logged off the datapad and took it next door to the examination room. "He's an herbalist. Does he know anything about starships?"

"No. I'm sure the others will make him run errands or clean anything that needs it. He'll love that." Jing rolled her eyes.

Nikki set the datapad on her mother's desk. "We should type up the patient files whenever we have some free time."

"Solona might need an official report to share with the Medics Guild. I could write one." Jing leaned against the exam table and rubbed her eyes. "Ms. Vaughn's party ran late. Do you think I could go back to the apartment for a nap?"

Nikki frowned. "I was going to ask you to watch the shop while I go with Corban to West Fort."

"Is he joining Thane's communication team?"

"He's not sure yet. He's still interested in becoming an herbalist."

"Then he needs to stay in Lakeside so we can train him, especially while *Baba*'s distracted with the *Unity* repairs."

"Sounds great to me, but he needs a place to live." Nikki noted Jing's smirk and wagged a finger at her before she could open her mouth. "Don't even think about it! It's still Mom's apartment!"

Jing pretended to be offended, although the eye-roll spoiled the effect. "I was going to say, 'We need someone like Ms. Vaughn in Lakeside.'"

"You expect me to believe that?" Nikki headed back to the main shop, with Jing on her heels. "I know you'd smuggle Thane over here in a heartbeat if you could find a place to hide him."

"He's too big to hide." Jing cackled. "I know, I've tried."

"He couldn't squeeze behind Ms. Vaughn's couch?" Nikki found a cloth to wipe down the long counter.

"How'd you guess?"

Nikki paused mid-wipe and turned to her friend. "I'm serious. Do you have any idea where Corban could live in Lakeside?"

"*Baba* has a two-bedroom apartment all to himself now. Too bad he thinks Strays are trashbird droppings."

"You want to hide him in your room?" Nikki started to laugh and couldn't stop as she imagined Corban hiding under Jing's old bed whenever Kun Kaczenski walked into his apartment.

"It worked for you. *Baba* never knew you were there." Jing joined in the laughter. "Maybe Corban could sleep here in the shop. We'll tell Solona"—she held her sides—"we're using him for practice, like a cadaver that's not quite dead."

Both were still howling with mirth when Corban walked into the shop, carrying a duffle bag. Jing took one look at him, snorted, and dashed back to the exam room.

"Is she all right?" Corban asked Nikki.

His expression was so genuinely perplexed that Nikki had to turn away so she could pull herself together. She wiped her eyes on the backs of her hands and took a few deep breaths. "I think she just had to pee."

"Yes, it was an emergency!" Jing called, sending both young women into gales of laughter again.

"I wish I knew what the joke was." Corban approached Nikki, but she held up a hand to ward him off.

"I need a moment." She was able to curtail the giggles and cleared her throat. "We were just discussing where you could live in Lakeside and got a bit carried away."

He flashed the chipped-tooth grin that always made her insides flutter. "I'd sleep in a tent in the marketplace if it meant I could stay near you."

"I'm not sure Mayor Brooks would approve that."

Corban's smile faded. "Well, until we find someone here willing to take me in, I need to head back to West. Thane's expecting me."

Nikki reached out to embrace him. He dropped his bag and wrapped both arms around her waist. The light that filled her mind was becoming an addiction. It renewed her soul as thoroughly as good food renewed her body when she was hungry. The thought of not seeing him every day was almost unbearable. His mouth found hers, and for several minutes, she forgot about everything, lost in the warm, calming oasis of Corban's light. *I don't want you to go.*

I don't want to go either.

Jing cleared her throat, startling them. "Sorry to interrupt the saliva swap, but three customers are on the porch and about to open the door."

Nikki drew back with reluctance, but kept a firm grip on Corban's free hand. *I'll try to find you a place to live in Lakeside.*

Corban nodded. *My ride is leaving. I know you wanted to go with me but you're needed here. I'm sorry. I'll miss you.*

I love you. She didn't mean to think it, but there it was, impossible to deny when he could sense exactly what she was feeling. Corban seemed startled but nodded and let go of her hand so fast she suspected he didn't want her to hear his response. She was disappointed, but understood his reluctance to reciprocate. The *L* word was a source of heavy expectations.

The bell on the door jingled, signaling a definite conclusion to their tender moment.

"Goodbye, Nikki." Corban retrieved his bag, turned around, and slipped by the three women near the door to exit the shop.

Nikki hoped her face wasn't red as she greeted the customers with a lackluster, "Good morning. How can we help you today?"

FIFTEEN
BRIDA'S PROGRESS

Thane was awakened by a voice in his head. *I need two metal-smiths to assemble range hoods in Brida's kitchen.* He pried his eyes open and looked around his bedroom. The curtains in front of the window filtered the light from Ilios, but it was still bright enough in the room to make him squint. From the incessant growling of his stomach, Thane figured it was midday.

We have sheet metal, laser torches, welding masks, and everything you need here. Could you and Rupert come today? We'd like to get this kitchen finished.

Rupert was snoring in the hammock parallel to Thane's, a muscular, freckled arm draped across his eyes. Corban occupied a third hammock near the window, but he was awake and poring over yet another book on herbal remedies.

Thane extended his right leg and nudged Rupert's hammock. "Wake up, Rhubarb. Derek needs us at Fort Brida."

"Why?" Rupert grunted without opening his eyes.

"Because he needs people who know how to weld." Thane climbed out of his hammock and strapped on his brace. When Rupert resumed his snoring, Thane gave his hammock a vigorous shake.

"What?" Rupert sat up too fast, and his hammock flipped over, dumping him onto the floor.

Corban and Thane roared with laughter. "Are you awake now?" Thane asked, feigning innocence.

"I've done that too many times." Corban climbed down from his own hammock and offered Rupert a hand.

"I think I broke my tailbone." Rupert pouted but allowed Corban to help him up.

"I hope not. That'll make the bike ride to Brida really painful," Thane said.

Rupert winced and rubbed his backside with both hands. "Next time, just yell in my ear, Stumpy."

Thane's reply was unsympathetic. "Get dressed. Let's get moving." He turned to his brother. "Let Zhao and Isaac know we might not be back until tomorrow, depending on how much work Derek has for us."

"They're still working on the kitchen?" Rupert went to the dresser for a T-shirt.

"I think they've made great progress in two months." Thane found his bluedeer-skin boots amidst the piles of dirty clothes scattered around the floor and pulled them on. "Ready?"

"Have fun," Corban said. "I'm leaving for Lakeside in a few minutes."

Since being released from the infirmary, his brother had been using Rupert's bike several days a week to travel to and from Lakeside's apothecary. Thane tried not to feel jealous of how much time Corban spent with Nikki, but it was difficult. Since Corban declined the offer to join the Sentries Guild, he was free to apply to another guild. He refused to be deterred by the fact that Jing's father wouldn't allow him to sit for the apprenticeship application test.

"Solona will find a way to make it happen," Corban had told him. "I have confidence in her."

Corban's commutes to Lakeside always made Thane uneasy. "Just stay away from—"

"The bridge," Corban and Rupert finished in unison. "Yes, Mother, I know." His brother rolled his eyes.

Thane shot him a warning frown before leaving through the door to the hallway. Rupert followed, still complaining that his butt hurt. "Do you whine this much to Yasmin?" Thane asked.

"Do you think I send her those kinds of messages?" Rupert flashed his lopsided grin. "She hears nothing but poetry from me every day. 'But soft, what light through yonder window breaks? It is the east, and Juliet is the sun.'"

"*Every day*? She'll be ready to wrap a tourniquet around your neck!"

Rupert shrugged. "We'll see. Hey, could we get something to eat first? I'm starving."

"Yes, but let's get it to go."

"Easy for you to say. You don't have to pedal the bike with a whole sandwich stuffed in your mouth."

"I could feed you if you like, Mr. Dainty Buttocks."

Rupert glared at him. "No, thanks."

They descended the stairs to the street and walked over to the dining hall. The place was nearly empty after the lunch hour rush, but Gina Piroux gave them a thumbs-up from the kitchen doorway.

"Derek told me Dagmar's waiting for you two, so I'll box up some leftovers."

"Thanks, Madam Mayor." Rupert settled into a chair at one of the tables and Thane sat across from him.

While they waited, Thane decided to eavesdrop on the kitchen staff. He was able to hone in on an interesting conversation between two teenage Normals assigned to kitchen duty. The pair was back in the walk-in refrigerator, gathering ingredients for the dinner menu.

"Fifteen heads of cauliflower." The young woman was reading from a list.

"Thirteen, fourteen," the young man reported. "One short."

"Close enough. Now we need onions."

"Red, yellow, or Vidalia?"

"It doesn't say. Yellow, I guess," she said. "No, that's garlic. Those big ones, bottom shelf. Did your dad really volunteer for the *Unity*'s crew?"

"He did, but my aunt is begging him not to go. She believes Mayor Piroux's warning about the explosion."

"I can't believe Corban Abrams can see the future. He didn't mention the ship landing here."

The young man's reply was thoughtful. "You expect him to see every event, for the entire colony?"

"Well, why wouldn't he?"

"That's not how clairvoyance works."

"How would you know? You're a Normal."

"I know a little bit about Talents. My cousin's a Stray. She's telepathic, but she can't hear everyone's thoughts. She has to concentrate on a single person, and they have to be standing near her for it to work. There are limits to any Talent, including Corban's."

"So you're saying he can only foresee certain events?"

"Yes. He has premonitions in his dreams, and no one can control their dreams. Is this enough onions?"

"Grab five more. How can he tell a regular dream from a premonition?" she asked.

"I'm sure he has enough experience with them to know the difference."

"What's stopping him from making up a story to scare people, like with this explosion?"

"He could, but what would be the point? He had nothing to gain by sharing this with the mayors, but the colony has a lot to lose if he's telling the truth. People, including my dad, could die. Corban's not trying to scare people, he's trying to save lives."

"My mom doesn't believe in premonitions. She'd like to go on the ship, but Chaim Rajamani said all the pods have been claimed."

No doubt by the highest bidders, Thane thought.

"Dad wanted me to go too, but Vesta's my home." Thane heard a distinct sniffle. "If the premonition's true, he'll die. Even if it's not true, I'll never see him again."

"I'm sorry." The young woman sounded sincere, although her sentiment was tainted by her next remark. "We need eighteen liters of tomato sauce."

Thane returned his attention to the dining room as Mayor Piroux set two reusable boxes on the table. "Here's the last of the barbeque bluedeer, coleslaw, and corn on the cob. Enjoy."

I can't eat that while steering the bike. Rupert raised an eyebrow at Thane.

"Thank you, ma'am." Thane grabbed the warm boxes and got to his feet. "We'll be sure to enjoy this as soon as we get to Fort Brida."

But I'm hungry now!

"Keep it up," Thane said as soon as the mayor returned to the kitchen, "and I'll tell Yasmin what a big baby you are."

"I suspect she already knows." Rupert smirked.

***

Thane managed to maintain a firm grip on the bicycle handles while keeping a food box tucked beneath each arm, although Rupert complained every half kilometer. "My food's going to smell like armpits."

By the time they took the right fork just past the bridge to Waterfall, Thane had reached his tolerance limit. "You're getting on my nerves. Maybe it was a bad idea for us to room together."

"I'd move back in with my mom if she wasn't such a nag." His friend switched to a falsetto voice. 'Why don't you ever come see me? You need to get married. I want grandbabies. You'd be more attractive to potential girlfriends if you'd cut your hair.'"

Thane laughed. "You sound just like her."

"I've told her a dozen times I *have* a girlfriend."

"That's news to me."

"Yasmin loves my poetry. And she likes my hair long."

Thane snorted. "If you say so."

"Maybe I'd be less whiny if our job wasn't so boring," Rupert said. "I miss being a metal-smith."

"I do too, sometimes, but Chaim's not going to let us back in the guild."

"The interment gave him the perfect excuse to ban us, even with Piroux warning him he can't discriminate against capable guild members."

"As if he'd ever listen to her," Thane said. "You realize Chaim didn't know you were a Stray until the roundup?"

"I hated hiding my Talent, but what can you do when your boss is a bigot? Zhao said his old man would probably kick Nikki out of the herbalists if Solona wasn't next in line for guild master. He didn't know Nikki was a Stray until she and Corban stole his truck during the roundup. Now he's furious Solona put Nikki and Jing in charge of Lakeside's apothecary."

"And they're doing a great job." Thane couldn't help smiling at the mention of Jing. "Kun should've done his job if he didn't want a Stray in charge of the shop. I don't think he's done anything for the guild since the *Unity* landed. Solona should be Herbalists Guild Master."

"Medics Guild Master too."

Thane struggled to stay balanced as the bike hit a rough patch in the road. "One person can't be in charge of two guilds."

"There's always a first time. Solona could handle it."

The forest soon gave way to open pastures. Rupert took the left fork when the road divided again. The last three kilometers to Fort Brida was a particularly rough stretch of road, with no gravel to smooth out the muddy ruts.

"Look at that," Thane said when the walls of the smallest fortress came into view. "Windows!"

Thane's original view of Brida, almost three months ago, had been unsettling because there were no openings for windows in the exterior walls. He soon learned that Leighton Abrams had designed the place like a prison, and a primitive one at that. The rooms that made up the exterior walls were windowless. Now rough holes had been gouged out of the stonework every ten meters along the perimeter, on the second and third levels.

"No glass. I'm glad they didn't try to poke holes on the main floor, not with all the night terrors we've been seeing. That would be an invitation to come on in and have a free dinner."

Thane silently agreed. He was grateful not to have sentry duty for one night.

Rupert steered the bike through the open gates and stopped next to the sentry station. Thane climbed off the handlebars and stretched his cramped legs, relieved the jarring ride was over. A sentry he didn't recognize nodded to them. He was impressed she was wearing a sidearm, the holster strapped to her right thigh. "Mayor Graham is expecting us," he told her. "Got any bullets in that?"

She nodded. "Full magazine, and I know how to use it. The night terrors have become more aggressive lately," she added, gesturing to a set of claw marks in the wooden gatepost on her left.

Rupert whistled softly. "I hope you're not guarding this place by yourself."

"Team of six for night duty." She tilted her head, indicating the direction of the communal kitchen. "You'll find Mayor Derek over there."

"Mayor Derek?" Thane smirked.

"He'd be happier if everyone dropped the 'mayor' part." She returned the smirk, winked at Rupert, who promptly turned pink, and waved them through the archway.

"Thanks." Thane led the way across the courtyard.

Rupert took one of the boxed lunches from him and opened the lid. He dug a fork from his back pocket and began shoveling shredded barbeque into his mouth as they walked.

"I guess the armpit smell isn't strong enough to curb your appetite?" Thane was too distracted by the dramatic changes to the fort to start on his own lunch.

The dirt compound had been cleared of cooking fires and latrine tents, replaced by several picnic tables, clotheslines, a large chicken coop, and a few well-tended gardens. The well was enclosed inside a shed. The stone kitchen was a finished one-story building, complete with a ceramic tile roof, although there was still a large fire pit just outside the main entrance.

Thane opened the door and held it for Rupert. Both young men stepped across the threshold and gawked at the neat dining room.

"Looks like they had plenty of help from the Carpenters Guild," Rupert said.

"And the Electricians Guild." Thane nodded approvingly at the overhead lights.

"Yes, and the plumbers helped too," Derek said as he burst through the swinging door to the kitchen. He shook hands with Thane and Rupert. "Thanks for coming."

"Nice work, Mr. Mayor," Thane said. "The place looks very different from when we left."

Derek shrugged, although he grinned at the praise. "Elie's just happy we finally have a working bathroom."

"I'd like a tour when we're done here." Thane followed Derek into an impressive commercial-grade kitchen, complete with three sink areas, two long prep counters, several refrigerators, and two iron stoves with large griddles. "Where did you get the ranges?"

"The *Unity* had one that needed assembling, but Mayor Piroux brought us the second." Derek grinned. "I have no idea where she got it, and I didn't dare ask."

"She boosted a spare from one of the other forts?" Rupert walked in behind Thane, still shoveling food into his mouth.

"Your words, not mine." Derek pointed out the wiring over the ranges and the exhaust pipes. "Dagmar is eager to start cooking indoors. I have to admit I'm tired of salads and campfire cuisine. Come on, I'll show you what needs to be done."

The mayor led them past a walk-in pantry to a back door. They stepped out into a narrow alleyway between the kitchen and fortress wall. Stacks of sheet metal, strips of solder, laser torches, grinders, cutters, C-clamps, files, and safety equipment, including gloves and welding masks, were piled on a blue tarp on the ground. "Caliper." Derek handed the measuring device to Thane. "There's a ladder around here somewhere. I'll track it down."

"Looks like you have everything," Rupert said. "I'm impressed. Not many people know what supplies welders need."

"It all came from the *Unity*," Derek said, "organized neatly in shipping containers, with instructions on paper."

"We'll get to work as soon as I inhale my lunch," Thane said.

Derek grinned. "I'd say no rush, but Dagmar wants to start dinner in two hours. It'll be nice to eat something without ashes in it."

"We'll do our best," Thane said.

There's no way we can build them in two hours, Rupert said. *Maybe two days.*

***

172

Thane stepped back, pleased with his work. The freshly welded range hood was a seamless fit for the ventilation fan. Now all it needed was an electrician to hook up the wiring and test it. Although he and Rupert didn't finish their work in time for dinner preparations, Dagmar didn't seem to mind.

"That looks great," she said from the nearest sink, where she was washing the cutting boards. The rest of her staff had already completed their chores, working around Thane and Rupert to do so, and had gone home. They were the only three left in the kitchen.

"You two hungry?" Dagmar asked.

"Starving." Rupert moved the ladder away from the range hood on the other side of the room. "But I think we need to wash up first."

"Yes, I can smell you from here." Dagmar grinned. "I'll show you to the guest suite."

"Brida has a guest suite?" Rupert's eyes widened.

Thane started gathering his tools, but the cook said, "Just leave them until morning. It's late, and I know you're tired."

"And hungry," Rupert reminded her.

Dagmar laughed and stripped off her purple apron. "I wish you had an older brother, Rhubarb. You're adorable."

Thane laughed too as Rupert's face turned as red as his hair. "I have an uncle who's single if you don't mind older men."

"Older?" Thane snorted. "Bertram's almost fifty."

"That's a bit too old for me, but if I get desperate, I'll let you know." Dagmar motioned for them to follow her out the back door.

They crossed the dark courtyard to the east wall. Dagmar opened door 15E and ushered them inside.

She flipped a switch next to the door and an overhead light came on.

"You've been busy." Thane's eyes skimmed the room, impressed. There were two twin beds neatly made with colorful quilts, one on either side of the window. A braided rag rug covered the floor between the beds, and a sturdy-looking wardrobe filled the space opposite the window, which faced the courtyard. "Two months ago I was sleeping on the floor in a windowless room. It was like being in a prison cell."

"People work fast when they're motivated to create better living conditions. Now you have the luxury of a window and a bathroom." Dagmar opened a newly framed door to the adjoining space, which had the basics installed: sink, toilet, and a one-piece shower stall. "The water doesn't heat after dark, but there might be enough in the tank for two quick showers. There are towels and toiletries in the wardrobe."

"You have plumbing!" Rupert was wide-eyed.

"Thanks to the *Unity*'s supplies and twenty Strays from the Plumbers Guild, yes, we have running water. We've been building bathrooms by putting up a wall in the middle of a room, closing off the doorway to the hall, then adding new doorways to the rooms on either side," Dagmar explained. "It's not as nice as having an apartment but it's much better than the original floor plan. We've only finished a third of the interior rooms. The exterior rooms will take much longer."

"Yes, we noticed the lovely windows on our way in." Thane grinned.

"Our stone masons all went back to Orchard Valley," Dagmar said. "So far we've discovered that sledge hammers don't make neat openings. We've been using the exterior rooms for storage because nobody wants to live in a windowless room."

"You got that right." Rupert shuddered.

"How many Strays are still in Brida?" Thane asked.

"Four hundred and fifty-six." Dagmar laughed at Thane's astonished face. "We keep track of everyone with the spreadsheet. The ones still here are from Waterfall, Greenfield, and East Fort."

"The anti-Stray forts." Rupert nodded as he sat on one of the beds to take off his boots.

Thane noted Dagmar's sudden frown. "You don't want to go back to West Fort?"

"No. My mom's done her best to shelter me from prejudice since the Plague, but I think it's past time I lived on my own. I'm head cook here, and I love it." She smirked. "Plus, it's nice not hearing the 'I want grandchildren' mantra several times a day."

"Same here," Rupert said.

"Thanks for the guest accommodations, Dagmar." Thane plopped down on the bed opposite Rupert's to take off his own boots.

She grinned over her shoulder as she opened the door to leave. "Derek and Solona are the ones you should thank. They've organized this place in record time. I guess all Brida lacks now is a school, but since the oldest second-generation Stray is only two, I don't think we'll need to worry about that for a few storms."

"Aren't some of the Strays still in school?" Rupert asked.

"A handful of sixteen-storms, but they'd all rather do hands-on training as apprentices." Dagmar shrugged. "Now if we only had some guild masters to train them. I'll be back in fifteen minutes with some food."

"Thanks!" both young men called after her as she pulled the door shut to their room. A brief scuffle ensued to see who'd get to the shower first, and Rupert won, slamming the bathroom door in Thane's face.

"Short shower! You'd better leave me some hot water!" Thane said.

Rupert responded with an evil cackle and turned on the water full blast.

SIXTEEN
NIKKI'S ERRAND

"Business has been slow this morning, so now would be a good time for me to go the library." Nikki's nonchalant announcement drew immediate and loud responses from Jing and Corban.

"Darkness! You *are not* going to the landing strip!" Jing spun around, almost dropping the datapad she'd been using to enter patient charts. The contents of Solona's desk were spread out over the large surface of the compounding lab table in front of her.

"You can't. It's too dangerous!" Corban dropped the pestle into the mortar he was using to crush coriander seeds. His work occupied the only free edge of the table, opposite Jing. "There's no reason to risk—"

"Sorry, but there's a good reason, and it's for you." Nikki leaned against the doorframe. "You've studied every book on Earth herbs we have in the shop. Now you need the file on Vesta's plants." When he opened his mouth to protest, she added, "You can't become an herbalist without that information. It'll all be on the apprenticeship test."

"Kun won't let me sit for the test," Corban said, "but that's not the point. You know it's—"

"—dangerous to go, especially alone," Jing finished for him.

"Kun might not be guild master much longer if he continues to neglect his duties, so you could take the test sooner than you think." Nikki did her best to project calm. She had already worked through all the objections she could think of before making her announcement. "I can't wait until we close the shop at dusk for Jing to go with me. As long as you stay here, there won't be any explosions."

"I'll go," Jing said. "There are too many Survivors working on the *Unity*, including our fathers. You don't want to risk running into them."

Nikki had been expecting this argument too. "You don't handle confrontations well. I'm not afraid of Kun or Elian. I'll take my sword."

Corban's brow furrowed. "That's like advertising that you're looking for trouble." He moved closer, but she held up a hand to ward him off.

"I'll be quick. I just need to copy the file." She reached for the datapad in Jing's hand. "I'll take that." To Corban she said, "Stay here and help her with any customers."

Jing smacked her palm on the table top. "Why are you being unreasonable? It makes more sense for me to go. The last time you snuck off somewhere by yourself, you ended up a prisoner in West's kitchen cellar."

"That was different. The slime worm who caught me is dead now." She exchanged a meaningful glance with Corban. "No one's going to give me any trouble for a quick trip to the library."

"Why are you so determined to go alone?" Corban tried again to intercept her.

Nikki managed to avoid him by snatching the datapad from Jing and hurrying back into the shop. "Just trust me." She took her sword from a cabinet beneath the long counter and armed herself in the usual way, with the blade through a belt loop. She managed to wedge the datapad into a cargo pocket on her jeans and was out the door.

The truth was Nikki wanted to see for herself what was happening with the *Unity*. It was reckless to look inside the ship, which is why she was determined to go alone. The herb file had been a plausible excuse. She planned to download it, but she also intended to take a detour afterward. *It's easier to ask forgiveness than permission, especially when my boyfriend's empathic.*

It was a short two kilometer walk around Gray Lake to the wide bridge, so Nikki didn't expect to run into any problems. Vehicle and pedestrian traffic was minimal around midday, with only a few delivery trucks on the road. Her heart rate sped up when she reached the concrete bridge to the landing strip.

She tried not to think about the premonition as she crossed the Cold River, but it was difficult to quell a feeling of panic when she caught sight of the *Unity*. *They smoothed out the giant dent.* It must have been difficult, given that the nose cone was at least eighty meters off the ground. *Did they work on it from inside the ship?*

Nikki reached the end of the bridge and walked past the Shrine. There were four trucks parked near the staircase to the *Unity*, but no one was outside the ship. She thought the blue Mechanics Guild truck belonged there, but the trucks of the farmers, herbalists, and merchants did not. She knew who'd driven the Farmers Guild vehicle and intended to avoid him, if possible.

She wondered how to look around inside the ship without being seen. *I wonder if Dagmar can make herself invisible.* With that random thought, Nikki continued across the cracked tarmac to the library ship to complete her legitimate errand.

Nikki tapped in the public access code on the keypad next to the airlock door and waited for it to rotate open. Once inside the bare antechamber, she waited for the round door to close behind her before climbing the main ladder to the fourth level. As usual, the room was unoccupied. Three round study tables, a few threadbare couches, and six holographic computer stations built into a bulkhead wall made up the entire library.

She crossed the dusty floor to one of the stations that still had working voice command. Sinking into the rickety chair in front of the monitor, she searched for an outlet to plug in the datapad. She was chagrinned to realize the technology was from different eras; the port on the terminal was a different shape than the one on the datapad. With the colony's satellite offline for nearly a decade, sending files wirelessly wasn't an option. She shoved the datapad back into her pocket. *So much for copying the file.* She gnawed her lower lip, thinking. *Printer?*

The library had a working printer, but paper was never provided, due to its scarcity. Nikki hadn't brought any paper with her. Having spent a great deal of time on the ship when Corban, Thane, and Zhao had gone into hiding here before the roundup, she knew there wasn't a scrap of paper anywhere.

How big is the file? Could I just type it? "Search: Native Plants of Vesta-Lambda," she instructed the monitor.

Lines of text filled the blue screen. The file was twenty-four pages, too long to type by hand, but small enough for a printed copy, provided she could find any paper. Even if she shrank the font to barely legible, she needed at least six sheets.

I wonder if there's paper in any of the trucks. It was a crazy idea, but she needed a copy of the file to avoid the wrath of Corban and Jing. Nikki decided to risk it.

Exiting the library, she noticed there was still no one outside the *Unity*, but without Thane's Talent to hear if anyone was coming, she would have to be hyper vigilant to avoid getting caught.

She jogged over to the closest vehicle, the faded maroon Merchants Guild truck, ducking down beside it so she couldn't be seen from the *Unity*'s airlock fifteen meters from the ground. She raised her head enough to peer through the driver's side window into the cab.

Bunch of trashbirds. The seats and floor were covered with hand tools, food containers, work gloves, and general garbage. When Derek and Eliana had been members of the Merchants Guild, they bartered in useful items, including paper. *Whoever drove this truck wasn't a merchant.*

Nikki squatted and peered underneath the vehicle, gauging the distance to the next one, which belonged to the Farmers Guild. *No way will the old man have any paper.* She wasn't even sure he knew how to write. *Better check anyway.*

She ran to the green truck, having to crouch behind the hood to avoid being seen from the airlock. She listened for a minute before deciding it was safe to take a quick peek inside the cab. She slipped around to the passenger's side door.

A gray shipping box with *Unity* printed on the lid took up half the seat. Nikki stole a glance at the airlock before opening the door and lifting the lid. The box was filled with several valuable items, including light bulbs, hand tools, coils of copper wire, and a tablet of plain white paper. She grabbed the paper and eased the door shut, just as her father stepped outside the airlock opening of the *Unity*.

"Get away from there!" Elian Ramirez took the stairs three at a time, moving faster than she thought possible.

Nikki pivoted to face him and drew her sword, holding it in front of her like a shield. "I just need some paper." She was relieved to see he was unarmed, recalling what an itchy trigger finger he had. The fact that he shot Corban still made her furious.

"What are you doing here, Nikolasa? You little thief!" He advanced on her but stopped short of the point of the sword. "Put that down! You know you won't use it on your own father."

"You've never claimed me as a daughter, so don't start now. Don't underestimate me. I used this to kill Leighton Abrams, and I'm not afraid to use it on a slime worm like you!"

Kun Kaczenski appeared at the top of the stairs. "What's going on?"

"Nothing important." Elian sneered without turning his way. "Just caught a thief stealing supplies from my truck. A foolish girl who should've stayed in Brida with the other Strays."

Jonah DeKalb appeared next to Kun. He didn't say anything as he stared down at the scene, and Nikki didn't like that she was outnumbered.

"I was just leaving. Stay where you are." She glared up at the other two men. "All of you."

The second her eyes strayed from her father, he lunged at her. Nikki hadn't planned how to defend herself, but she instinctively swung the heavy sword at him. She struck his left shoulder, drawing blood.

Ramirez's scream was filled with both outrage and pain as he fell to his knees, covering the long gash with his right hand. "Darkness!" It appeared to be deep as blood gushed between his fingers, running down his arm. "Worthless Stray! You'll pay for this!"

"You're lucky I didn't chop it off!" Nikki shouted with more courage than she felt. She backed away, the tablet of paper still clutched in her left hand. "Stay away from me!"

Jing's father scowled as he descended the stairs and went to Elian's aid. "To think my daughter is friends with a violent Stray like you! You should all be locked up!"

"Two of a kind, aren't you?" she fired back. "Rejected your own children for being Strays? You're the ones who should be locked up!" Nikki put as much space as she could between the guild masters and herself.

When it seemed clear that none of the men intended to pursue her, she turned and sprinted back to the library ship, frustrated there was no way to barricade the airlock door behind herself. Her hands were shaking as she loaded paper into the printer and made a copy of the file. She folded the papers into quarters and crammed them into her cargo pocket with the datapad. *So much for getting a look inside the ship.*

Nikki had no idea how she would get past the *Unity* and return to Lakeside, not with a hostile group of Survivors on the tarmac, tending her father's injury and watching for her. She climbed to the seventh level where there was a port window in an empty cabin that had once belonged to the ship's captain. She could see the people on the tarmac if she craned her neck far enough to the right. She watched Kaczenski and DeKalb help her father walk to the hospital ship, which was on the other side of the library. Once they were out of sight, she returned her attention to the *Unity*.

There were six men and two women she didn't recognize gathered around the foot of the staircase. They all wore work coveralls and appeared to be discussing her altercation with Elian. At least, that's what she assumed since they kept glancing over at the library ship with angry faces. *Will they come after me?* And more important, *what should I do if they come after me?*

Nikki debated her limited options. She was stranded unless she could be brave enough or fast enough to run past the *Unity* to the wide bridge. Running the other direction, away from the *Unity*, wasn't an option because she'd never be allowed into East Fort. *Mayor Savoy would toss me right into a holding cell and throw away the key.*

There were other starships on the tarmac, but they had all been stripped to the girders. They offered shelter from the annual storm but little else in the way of facilities. At least the library had a few working bathrooms and one galley.

Jing and Corban will worry if I'm not back soon. She sat on the floor and drew her knees up to her chin. *I need to learn to control my curiosity. It's gotten me into so much trouble.*

If I stay here, who will search for me first, the old man or Jing? Both prospects worried her, and she didn't want Jing confronting Kun or Elian. Nikki was confident Corban wouldn't venture to the bridge, not with the premonition, *and not with me here, so close to the* Unity.

It would be nice to be able to send messages, like Rupert and Derek. Nikki was old enough to remember when the colony's coms still worked, before the technology wore out. She rubbed her left wrist, recalling the tiny unit she used to wear, a device that made it effortless to talk to anyone, anywhere on Vesta. Even with two cases of new com units from the *Unity*, the tech was worthless without a working satellite.

Now the only way to communicate with someone was to find them and speak in person, unless you were fortunate enough to have access to one of the twenty-six Strays who could send mental messages. Of course, receiving a message wasn't much use if you couldn't reply to the sender.

She grew weary of chasing her thoughts around and stood again to look out the window. Nikki came to the conclusion that her only option was to run for it if there was an opportunity, even if it meant waiting until all the workers went home for the evening. If anyone came onboard to search for her, her only choice would be to fight. She held up the sword, noted her father's dried blood on the blade, and wondered if the weapon would be enough protection. She recalled an old Earth saying, "Don't bring a knife to a gunfight." She wouldn't put it past Elian Ramirez to show up with a gun the next time they met.

Time crawled by. DeKalb and Kaczenski reappeared at the *Unity*'s staircase and ushered the others inside, except for one. A middle-aged man with dark skin and a stoic expression sat on the bottom step and fixed his gaze on the library ship airlock. Nikki was trapped.

Eventually she got hungry and climbed the ladder to the galley. A quick search of the cabinets and refrigerator came up short. A half-empty bottle of ketchup and a canning jar filled with cloudy, dill-scented brine but no pickles comprised the entire contents of the fridge. There was a loaf of bread in the freezer, but it was shrouded in a layer of ice. *Only if I'm about to starve to death.* She found a cup and filled it at the filtered faucet. The water from the ship's cistern had a weird metallic taste, but she was too thirsty to care.

Nikki returned to the window and kept vigil, waiting to see if her guard would grow impatient and go back inside. She also kept an eye on the bridge, hoping for a Stray posse to show up, but no one came.

Hours passed, the sky grew dim, and the Survivors working on the *Unity* stepped outside the airlock, manually rolled the door into place, and then climbed into the trucks and drove away.

Where's Elian? Since her father never reappeared, she wondered if he had to spend the night in the hospital. Secretly, Nikki hoped she'd done some serious damage to his shoulder. *After what he did to Corban, he deserves it.* At the same time, she wondered if she needed to keep an eye on the library's airlock to make sure he didn't try to ambush her.

She ignored her growling stomach, got another drink of water, and climbed down to the antechamber. The tiny port window in the airlock door revealed an abandoned tarmac and a sky rapidly growing darker.

This is my chance! She was in motion before she talked herself out of it.

Nikki opened the airlock, waited for it to close behind her, descended the gangway, and sprinted across the weed-choked asphalt to the *Unity*. She ascended the stairs and rolled the airlock door out of the way. It appeared heavy but rolled easily on its repaired track. Once inside the antechamber, she rolled the door shut. *And let's pray night terrors don't know how to open doors,* she thought breathlessly, seeing no way to lock it.

The lights in the ship were on motion sensors so the entryway lit up like midday. Nikki looked around the claustrophobic space at the white bulkhead walls, steel deck plates, and a dazzling array of panels, buttons, and switches. One access panel had been removed, the plate dangling from the complex wiring above it, evidence that work was still in progress.

She patted the hilt of her sword to make sure it was secure in her belt loop, and stepped to the ladder.

Nikki climbed slowly, taking in every detail of the strange ship. She got off on the next level and tried to recall what Thane described from the original scouting party report.

Stasis pods. She stared at the coffin-shaped steel boxes, arranged like bunk beds in five columns of four, creating a hexagon-shaped room with the doorway forming the sixth wall. The lids were open on each, with an array of brightly colored wires and tubes suspended from the tops and bottoms like electronic spaghetti. She approached the first one and peered inside, but the mechanical layout was incomprehensible. The thought of spending several storms inside one made her shudder.

Nikki started to step back when a white label on the edge of the lid caught her eye. A single name was printed on it: *Ramirez, Elian Volkov Macdonald.* She removed the datapad from her cargo pocket and recorded the name on each pod. The potential passengers were Stray-haters, and she knew what was going to happen to all of them if they forced this project to its tragic conclusion. She decided the colony might want to remember their names, as morbid as the idea seemed.

DeKalb, Jonah; Savoy, Mariposa; Kaczenski, Kun; Rajamani, Chaim. Yes, the gang's all here, Nikki thought, *except one.* She squinted to read the label on the top pod, fifth row, but it was blank. *Who's the unlucky soul who hasn't been chosen for this mission?*

SEVENTEEN
FEAR AND HOPE

"Where's Nikki?" Corban had been frantic a few times in his life, but this one topped them all. "She's been gone for hours! Something's happened to her!" The fears he'd repeated a dozen times over the course of the afternoon tumbled out in no particular order. "Someone has to go to the landing strip!"

Jing was almost in tears as she nodded and repeated her mantra, "There's nothing we can do! You can't go to the landing strip, and I can't leave you here to run the shop alone." She shut the door behind the last customer and flipped the sign to *Closed*. An endless stream of colonists had come through the apothecary all afternoon, making it impossible for her to leave.

"I could go now." She sounded uncertain. "I'll take Rupert's bike."

Corban glanced at the sky through the window. "It's almost dark. You can't leave the fort."

She turned on the waterworks in earnest, and he didn't know what to do. Comforting Jing was Thane's department. His mind cycled through an endless loop of possible outcomes to Nikki's errand—none of them good—but the fact that neither he nor Jing could search for her was the worst part.

"I should've gone back to West and asked Thane and Zhao to look for her." He hated himself for waiting too long, for assuming she'd be back, and especially for not telling her he loved her when he had the opportunity. *Don't assume the worst, don't assume the worst,* he chanted in his mind, trying to rein in his emotions.

He had a flashback to the night he'd found Nikki in the tiny cellar beneath West's kitchen pantry, her hands tied and her mouth taped. His vile uncle and the sentry O'Rourke had left her there all day, intending to send her outside the gates during the night. The only way Corban was able to find her was with the help of a premonition, a dream he'd had the night before, and from a timely message from Derek Graham, informing him Nikki was missing. His insides turned to ice at the thought of her being held prisoner again or, worse, trapped outside the fort at night.

"It's too late to go after her." Jing's voice cracked. "Nikki's smart; we have to assume she took refuge in one of the ships for the night. Maybe she's still in the library."

Corban bit his lip, trying not to give voice to what he really wanted to say. Shouting at Jing for not closing the shop earlier wouldn't help either of them. The fact remained that they didn't know where Nikki was, and they had no way to find her until morning.

"Thane will notice you didn't come back." Jing dug a handkerchief from her apron pocket and blew her nose.

"He won't come looking for me, if that's what you're worried about. Rupert will probably send me a message soon, telling me to stay put. Thane and I have an understanding about not searching for each other after dark."

He sensed her relief at his reply, but that reassurance did little to diminish the misery trickling down her face. "I don't know what to do!" Jing wailed. "I feel so helpless."

She was such an emotional mess that Corban put on a brave show for her sake. "There's nothing we can do tonight. Let's get something to eat—"

"I'm not hungry." Jing's face was blotchy-pink from crying.

He decided she must have a bottomless reservoir of tears. "I guess I could sleep on the couch in your apartment."

"I won't be able to sleep." Jing sniffled.

Corban sighed. "Let's go." He took the keys from her and locked the shop. They walked to Solona Zegarelli's in the dark. The lights shining from apartment windows offered some illumination as they traversed the cobbled streets.

"Key's on the ring," Jing said tonelessly when they reached 26S.

Corban opened the door, turned on the lights, and locked it behind them. He watched as Jing walked straight back to the bathroom and shut the door. The couch didn't look inviting, but he doubted he'd get any sleep anyway.

Jing emerged from the bathroom in flowery pink pajamas. "I don't think Nikki or Thane would care if you slept in her bed tonight. The couch is really uncomfortable. Trust me, I know." She walked back to the bedroom and stretched out on the twin bed to the left of the window.

Corban splashed water on his face at the bathroom sink, took off his boots, turned off all the lights, and lay down on the other bed. It was awkward sharing a room with Jing, so he rolled over to face the wall.

The pillow case smelled like Nikki. He breathed in the citrusy-sage scent, but this only sharpened his anxiety. *Where is she?* Although Corban hadn't been to church in several storms, he needed to do *something*. He shut his eyes and offered a short prayer for her safety.

Even with Jing's noisy sniffling on the other side of the room, a sense of peace gradually fill his mind until he was able to fall asleep.

***

Corban was back in Lakeside's infirmary, but this time he wasn't the patient. He was standing at the foot of his bed in front of the narrow window, but someone else was lying in it, sound asleep. None of the other beds were occupied. It was late, and the room was dark, illuminated by weak starlight through the single windowpane. He thought about turning on a lamp, but something made him hesitate. He had a feeling he shouldn't wake the patient.

He sensed peace and contentment, but it took him a few moments to realize those feelings weren't emanating from the patient. There was something warm cradled in his arms. He looked down and gasped. He was holding a newborn baby bundled in a soft blanket. All Corban could make out in the poor lighting was a tiny face looking up with great interest at him.

Corban tore his gaze from the infant's bright eyes and moved around the bedside to take a closer look at the patient.

It was Nikki. She was lying on her right side, her long black hair splayed across the pillow and a look of sheer exhaustion etched on her face.

Corban turned his attention to the newborn again, his mind unable to process the shock. *I'm holding my own child!*

***

"I'm not ready!" Corban sat straight up in bed, his heart pounding.

"Not ready for what?" Jing mumbled from the depths of her pillow. "What are you yelling about?"

"Nothing." He noted the strange feminine room, recalling where he was. "It was just a dream."

"Your dreams mean trouble." Jing sounded more awake. She sat up and blinked at the soft light of dawn streaming in through the window. "Did you have a premonition?"

"You don't want to know," he said honestly, rubbing his eyes. "But I do know one thing."

Jing swung her feet over the side of her bed. "What's that?"

Corban mustered a smile, the dream still fresh in his mind. "I know Nikki will be all right."

"I wish I had a Talent like yours." Jing's tone was filled with hope.

"No, you don't." Corban got to his feet and searched for his boots. "Let's get to the landing strip."

"Wrong! Did you hit your head during the night? You can't go! I'm going, just as soon as I brush my disgusting teeth." Jing dug some clothes out of the dresser and headed to the bathroom.

"You shouldn't go alone!" Corban called after her.

"I won't be alone. Thane, Zhao, and Rupert will be here in ten minutes—Rupert just informed me," she added before Corban could form a question. She closed the bathroom door in his face.

Corban dampened a clean dish towel at the kitchen sink and used it to wash his face. He found a spearmint plant on the window sill and broke off a leaf, stuck it in his mouth, and chewed until his breath was marginally fresher. He spat out the leaf in the trash and pulled on his boots.

Jing was out of the bathroom in five minutes, looking surprisingly polished for someone who spent half the night crying, but he suspected she'd spruced up for Thane's benefit. "Let's hurry to the gates to meet them," she said.

They walked to the door but stopped short, their eyes drawn to the floor. A folded slip of paper was lying near the threshold. Corban experienced a flutter of panic as his imagination took over, thinking it was a ransom note, but Jing picked it up and unfolded it.

"It's to me. It's from *Baba*."

Corban breathed a mental sigh of relief. "What's it say?"

Jing scowled. "He wants to see me. I'm supposed to meet him at his apartment tomorrow after dinner." She snorted in disgust and tossed the paper aside. "He's says it's urgent." She opened the door and stepped into the hallway but turned to face Corban, her mood instantly shifting from angry to hopeful. "I'm so relieved you know Nikki's safe. I wish you'd told me last night."

"Last night I didn't know." Corban pulled the door shut, locked it, and pocketed the key ring. "And I didn't say she was safe, I said I know she'll be all right. I had a premonition."

"I knew it!" Jing led the way downstairs to the street level. "Tell me."

"I can't." Corban frowned as they walked quickly toward the gates. "I can't even tell Nikki about this one. Not for several storms."

Jing laughed. "I'll be sure to nag until you confess."

"Sorry I mentioned it."

The night sentry was just opening the gates. A purple Cooks Guild truck sped into the fort as soon as there was enough space between the tall doors for it to pass. Rupert and Zhao waved to them from the truck bed.

Thane was driving. He stopped in front of Jing and Corban and flung himself from the cab. "What happened? Where've you been?" He glared at his brother.

"I've been here, obviously," Corban said. "Long story, but we need to find Nikki. She went to the library yesterday and didn't come back."

Jing ambushed Thane, with open arms, before Corban finished explaining. His brother lifted her off her feet, kissing her long enough to make everyone uncomfortable. "We need to find Nikki!" Corban reminded the amorous duo.

"Yes, please keep the slobber-fest to a minimum, *mei mei*." Zhao rolled his eyes. "I'd like to keep my breakfast down."

Thane set Jing on her feet and ushered her inside the cab.

"Open the shop if you feel comfortable waiting on people," Jing told Corban. "If not, just stay around here. We'll be back as soon as we find her."

Corban was anxious to go with them, but he didn't have a choice. "Keep me informed," he told Rupert, who gave him a lazy thumbs-up.

Thane climbed into the driver's seat, did a U-turn, and left through the gateway. Corban watched the purple truck until it drove out of sight. He shoved his hands into his pockets and started toward the dining hall, his mind a whirl.

He'd witnessed a scene from his future with Nikki. The thought of his latest premonition filled him with terror and joy at the same time. *Me, a father?* Suddenly "shared light" took on an entirely new meaning.

His pleasant thoughts were cut short as he walked into the dining hall and came face-to-face with Kun Kaczenski.

The Herbalist Guild master glared at Corban. "You have no business at the apothecary! You will never be allowed to take the apprenticeship test!"

"Nice to see you too, sir." Corban didn't try to keep the sarcasm out of his tone. "I'll be sure to tell Jing and Zhao hello for you."

Kun snarled and tried a new threat. "You tell your brother to stay away from my daughter!"

Corban was secretly pleased to sense that this unexpected meeting had thrown the Survivor off his guard. "That's going to be difficult since they just left the fort together, but I'll be sure to pass along your concerns."

"Worthless Stray! It'll be a relief to leave this place and get away from all of you!" Kaczenski pushed past him and stomped out the door.

"Have a nice day!" Corban called after him. He heard a smattering of applause and looked around in surprise at the Strays seated in the dining area or standing at the buffet table.

"You tell that arrogant trashbird!" someone called.

"Good job, Corban!" Alfredo and Nehal Hong raised their orange juice glasses, as if to toast him.

"Come join us," Nehal added. "Alfredo needs to hear your premonition again."

Corban experienced a flutter of panic as his thoughts flew to last night's dream, but then he realized she was referring to the pending explosion at the landing strip. "Just as soon as I get a plate. I'm starving."

EIGHTEEN
PASSENGER TWENTY

Thane couldn't figure out how to put his arm around Jing and safely drive the truck with one hand, but she solved the dilemma by hugging his right bicep and resting her head against his shoulder.

"Nikki got this crazy idea to go to the library ship to copy the file of Vesta's native plants for Corban, and she took off before either of us could stop her," Jing explained in one breath. "She didn't come back, and we had too many customers, so I couldn't close the shop, and Corban and I started to get scared. But then it got dark, and there was nothing we could do—"

"All right, slow down. I'm sure she's still in the library."

"But why wouldn't she come back?" Jing asked. "It should've only taken her an hour, at most. She must've run into someone from the *Unity*. She'd never deliberately do anything to make me or Corban worry. All I could think about was the time your uncle locked her up in the cellar, and I don't think I slept at all last night—"

"Calm down." Thane tried again to intercept her runaway mouth. "We'll be there in five minutes. I'm sure she's fine."

"*Baba* put a note under the door last night." Jing switched topics without slowing her pace. "He wants me to meet him at his apartment tomorrow night. He said it's urgent."

Thane was uneasy at this announcement, knowing how manipulative Kun Kaczenski could be, especially when it came to the one person he truly loved: Jing. "Are you going to go?"

"I don't know. I haven't spoken to him since I moved out. Do you think I should?"

Thane wanted to tell her no, but he also knew she had to make her own decisions without feeling pressured. However, he did have one idea. "What if I listen in on your meeting? I could wait in Solona's apartment."

"Yes." She paused, her tone turning thoughtful. "Yes, I'd feel much safer if I'm not facing him alone. Thank you." She stretched to plant a kiss on his cheek. Her breath was warm against his ear as she whispered, "I love you."

He almost drove into the lake.

Zhao pounded on the back window as soon as Thane got the wheels back on the road. "Watch your driving, Abrams! It's bumpy back here!"

"Sorry!" Thane could feel his face heating up as Jing snuggled his bicep again and giggled.

A minute later they reached the wide bridge. Thane took a deep breath and kept driving, ignoring the panicked little voice in his head that screamed at him to stop. *Corban's not here. Nothing's going to explode today.*

He focused on the Shrine straight ahead and drove across the bridge. Once they reached the other side, he released a breath he didn't realize he was holding and drove toward the library.

Only one truck was parked near the *Unity*, so Thane wasn't worried about confronting any Survivors, not this early. He pulled up beside the library's gangway and turned off the engine.

Nikki opened the airlock door and rushed down the ramp before Thane could even step out of the cab. She threw herself in the passenger's side with a breathless, "Hello!" and "Let's go!"

"What happened?" Jing asked, hugging her.

"Tell you about it on the way," Nikki said, "but I'd really like to get out of here before Dad checks out of the hospital."

Thane resumed his seat and thumbed the ignition on. "Hospital? What's he doing—?"

"Long story, long night. I'm starved. Please, let's go." Nikki turned around in her seat to wave at a perplexed Rupert and Zhao in the truck bed. "Thanks for coming to get me."

She sounded so nervous that Thane didn't press for answers. He put the truck in gear and turned around.

In the fifteen minutes it took to drive back to Lakeside, Nikki talked nonstop, almost as fast as Jing. After describing her misadventures from yesterday, she emphasized that the *Unity* had been repaired.

"All systems are online, the AI is back, and the bridge is in pristine condition." With wide eyes and her mouth pinched into a thin, tight line, she turned her face toward Thane and Jing. "It's ready to launch."

***

"*Baba*, why did you ask me here?" Jing asked.

"I just want to talk. I've missed you." Kun Kaczenski's voice rang with false brightness Thane could detect, even from a distance.

"I have nothing to say to you."

"Nothing? Not even goodbye?" Kaczenski sounded hurt, but the faint undercurrent of malice in his tone made Thane uneasy. "We'll never see each other again."

"I tried to tell you that you'll die if you attempt to launch the *Unity*." Jing was pleading, all bravado gone. "Please listen to me. Corban saw it—"

"He's a *liar*!" Kaczenski roared, all trace of meekness gone. "That boy is full of mischief! Spreading ridiculous tales to manipulate others!"

"All his premonitions have come true! He saw Nikki in that orchard *before* he even met her! He's never been wrong!"

"You've turned against your own father for these lying friends of yours? These *Strays*?" He spat out the word as if it was the vilest profanity.

"You think Corban is a liar because he's a Stray?" Thane detected the dangerous chill in Jing's tone.

You've done it now. Thane almost felt sorry for the guild master. *She's going to eviscerate you with her words until you beg for mercy.*

"Stop this. Come, sit down," Kaczenski said. "Let's discuss this calmly, father to daughter."

"No father of mine would exile his own son like a common criminal!"

There was a scuffling sound, Jing hissed in anger or surprise, more scuffling, and something wooden crashed to the floor, like a chair.

"Let me go!" Jing gasped. "*Baba*, don't do this!"

Thane was on his feet, moving as fast as he could to the door. He had to close his eyes to concentrate on Jing's voice, making it impossible to see where he was going. He stubbed his toe on the doorframe and stumbled into the hallway. He opened his eyes just long enough to get his bearings, and then used the wall to guide his steps as he moved as fast as his leg would allow.

"I tried to reason with you," Kaczenski said, "but you refused. You've been brainwashed by the Strays."

Jing made a faint gurgling noise that terrified Thane. *What's he doing to her?* He tried to move faster, cursing his bad leg as he reached the turn to the east wall. The Kaczenski apartment was only one hundred meters down the corridor, but it felt like one hundred kilometers.

Thane stumbled and almost fell. He would have given anything to have a different Talent, to have Frieda's amplified voice or Rupert's ability to communicate thoughts to others. Nikki and Corban were in the apothecary, too far away to hear him if he screamed, which he really wanted to do.

He got his bearings again and shut his eyes, tuning his hearing even as he kept moving forward. He had to know what was happening to Jing.

"I'm sorry it has to be this way," Kun muttered, "but I will not leave my daughter behind."

Darkness! He's taking her on the ship! Thane heard a door open.

"I can carry her," Kun said.

There's someone else in the apartment?

"When she awakens, we'll be back on Earth, the home of our ancestors."

"Don't get sentimental," Chaim Rajamani's voice rang with derision. "Let's move."

"Help!" Thane abandoned what little restraint he had left and pounded on a door. When no one answered, he stumbled across the hall and banged his fists on another apartment. "Please help me!"

A woman threw the door open. She was older, a Survivor, her tanned face a mixture of shock and suspicion. "What's going on? Who are you?"

"Kun's abducting his daughter! Call the sentries! We have to stop him!" Thane didn't wait for a response but continued down the hall, with his eyes open, desperate to reach 28E. "Please help me!" he bellowed over his shoulder, in case the woman didn't get the message.

Several more doors flew open, and residents poked their heads out, looking around in alarm.

"What's going on?"

"What's all the shouting?"

"Is there a fire?"

"Who needs help?"

"I do!" Thane was frustrated there was no time to explain. All he could do was pray someone took action. "Tell the sentries to block the gates!"

He was a few meters from Kaczenski's apartment when the door flew open and Chaim stepped into the hallway. The burly Smiths Guild master faced Thane, a sinister smile on his face.

"Don't listen to this man!" he shouted at the confused spectators spilling into the hallway from their apartments. "He's trying to stop Kun from getting his daughter to the hospital!"

Thane's heart skipped a beat as Kun stepped into the hall behind Chaim, a limp Jing gathered in his arms. "No! He's abducting her!"

"She's very sick!" Chaim said. "If she doesn't get to the hospital soon, she'll die! This Stray's confused! He's delirious! Someone stop him!"

Someone did. Thane felt as if a truck hit him from behind. He hit the floor hard, pain exploding in his nose, chest, and left leg. The brace bit into his thigh as it was wrenched out of place.

"I've got him, guild master. Go!" Thane's heavy captor kept him pinned.

Thane's nose was bleeding from his impact with the floor, probably broken again, but he didn't care. He raised his chin, watching helplessly as the guild masters' backs shrank from view down the hallway. "Please, I'm telling the truth. You have to let me go."

"I'll let you up when they're gone," came the unsympathetic reply.

The crowd milled about, standing over him, arguing about what was really going on.

"Kaczenski hasn't spoken to his daughter in months. Maybe this man's telling the truth."

"I am!" Thane said. "Please stop them!"

"Never trust the word of a Stray," someone else muttered.

"What does it matter if he's a Stray?" a woman said angrily.

"What's going on here?" a distinct alto belted out.

Thane recognized Mayor Brooks's voice. He mustered the strength to raise himself onto his elbows. "Kun's taken Jing!" Blood pooled in his mouth, slurring his words. He spat it out and tried again. "Please, ma'am, you have to stop them!"

"Let him up!" Brooks said. "What's the matter with you people? Why don't you help him?"

The weight on his back was gone, and Thane struggled to his unsteady feet. His nose was gushing, but he ignored his shocked audience and turned to face the mayor. "Please, ma'am, have your sentries stop them! I'm begging you!"

"Hold on a moment, and tell me what's going on." She offered him a handkerchief and seemed surprised when he didn't take it. "I was just coming down from my office when I heard all the shouting—"

"There's. No. Time." Thane was shaking. His brace was loose, and he had to shift his weight onto his right leg to stay upright. "They're going to put her on the *Unity*. It's set to launch—"

Brooks shook her head, peering up into his face with skepticism. "The *Unity* won't—"

"It's going to explode! Corban saw it happen! Everyone on the *Unity* is going to die!" Thane's left leg gave way, and he fell onto his hands and right knee, tears mingling with the blood from his nose.

Thane realized exactly why he and Nikki were trying to reach the *Unity* with Corban in his premonition. He also knew they would be too late. "*Jing!*"

NINETEEN
RACE

"Something's wrong." Corban peered through the glass of the apothecary door, staring out at the mostly deserted marketplace.

Nikki stepped away from the counter where she was labeling a jar of something smelly. "What's wrong?"

"I don't know." Corban turned to face her. "It's just a feeling."

"Thane's eavesdropping on Jing's conversation with her father. She should be safe." Nikki caught Corban's eye, didn't seem to like what she saw in his expression, and reached into the cabinet beneath the counter to retrieve her trusty sword. She crossed the shop to his side and slid the blade through a belt loop on her left hip. "They're both safe?"

Corban shook his head. "I don't know why I have this feeling. I just know something's wrong."

Nikki took his hand. "Let's go." She flipped the window sign to *Closed*, stepped outside the shop with him, and locked the door.

He felt an urgency he couldn't explain. "Let's run."

Nikki hiked up her apron and led the way through the market, zigzagging between tents, sheds, and shoppers, heading toward the south wall.

No, head for the gates.

It was reassuring that Nikki didn't question him, mentally or verbally. The bond of trust they shared was incredible, but Corban didn't take time to wonder about it. All he knew was his sense of foreboding had kicked in hard.

They reached the street bordering the east wall, just in time to see two men racing beneath the archway to exit the fort. One of them was carrying something heavy in his arms.

Or someone. Corban gasped. *It's Jing!*

"Jing!" Nikki screamed.

The man carrying Jing glanced over his shoulder long enough for them to recognize Kun Kaczenski.

"Stop!" Corban yelled.

The man with Jing's father glanced over at them. It was Chaim Rajamani. He flashed an arrogant grin and rushed Kun through the gates. They were gone.

"Someone stop them!" Nikki dropped Corban's hand and sprinted after the men, the long sword bouncing against her thigh.

Corban tried to think. He scanned the street for a vehicle while he ran after Nikki. He spotted a Farmers Guild delivery truck parked in front of the dining hall and made a detour toward it. "Nikki! Come on, we can't catch them on foot!"

Well, maybe she can. Corban watched her tear past the gates without looking back. *Darkness. What's she going to do if she catches them?* Fresh fear urged him to move faster. He reached the truck and yanked open the driver's side door, thumbing the ignition on before he was in the seat.

"Hey!" A man was unloading a crate of celery from the truck bed. "What are you doing?"

"Sorry!" Corban hit the accelerator, and tires squealed as he peeled away from the building. "I need to borrow it! It's an emergency!" He drove full speed toward the gates, praying that no one wandered across his path before he could exit the fort.

He almost hit Thane, who burst from the east wall stairwell directly in front of him.

Corban stood on the brake pedal with both feet and yanked the wheel to the left, the bed of the truck skidding to a halt centimeters from Thane. "Are you *crazy*? I could've killed you!"

Thane threw himself in the passenger's seat. "Just drive!"

Corban did a double take at his brother's battered appearance. His shirt was stained bright red with blood, which was still pouring from both nostrils. Corban hit the accelerator again, too shocked to articulate a question.

"I tried to stop them." Thane leaned forward to work on the straps of his brace, which appeared to be twisted in the wrong direction. "I heard Kun drug her—he did something to knock her out—and ran as fast as I could, screaming for help."

Corban leaned on the horn, and an astonished Lakeside sentry scrambled out of the way. He threaded the gateway arch and urged the wheezing truck to go faster. He saw Nikki one hundred meters ahead, still running like a bluedeer down the road. She'd almost reached the lake, but there was no sign of Jing's abductors. "Your nose?"

"Some idiot tackled me. He let them get away." Thane's tone was bitter. He yanked open the glove box, rummaged through the contents, and extracted a small first aid kit. "I hope there's some gauze in here."

Corban focused on the road, trying not to break an axle on the uneven ruts. "Where are they?" From the corner of his eye, he saw Thane stop blotting his nose long enough to focus his hearing.

"They had a truck waiting outside the fort." There was a catch in his voice. "They've already reached the landing strip. I hear a mechanical voice . . . counting down."

Corban's mouth went dry. "We're not going to reach them in time."

"No." Thane's tone was bleak. "No, we're not. Just like you saw in your premonition."

The truck drew alongside Nikki, and she slowed to a jog. She drew her sword before throwing herself in the passenger's side, crowding Thane to the middle of the cab.

"They had a truck," she panted, her face damp with perspiration and tears. She set the sword down, gripped the hilt between her knees, and took some deep breaths.

"We know." Thane's voice cracked. Corban sensed he was close to an emotional breakdown.

Nikki stripped off the apron, which had bunched around her hips, and pressed it over Thane's nose. "Lean your head back and pinch it here."

"It doesn't matter." Thane made no effort to take the apron from her. "We're too late."

Corban sensed a dramatic shift in Nikki's emotions. She gripped Thane's shoulder with her free hand and actually shook him. "It's only too late if you've given up! Would Corban be here if you thought it was too late to save him from the night terror? *No!* Would Corban be here if I thought I couldn't reach the orchard in time? *No!*"

She leaned toward Thane, a crazed expression on her beet red face and her lips peeled back in a snarl. "There's always a missing piece to Corban's premonitions! We *don't know* if Jing's on the *Unity* when it blows up! *We. Don't. Know.* I'm not giving up on my best friend, not when we're close enough to rescue her!"

"Darkness. You don't have to scream at him," Corban muttered, stunned to witness this feral side of Nikki.

"No, she's right." Thane took the apron from her and pressed it against his nose. He drew in a shuddering breath. "I lost my nerve for a minute. It's not over yet."

"There'll be time to mourn later." Nikki swiped at her own watering eyes. "Maybe," she added in a whisper. "I'm sorry I shook you and shouted at you."

"Apology accepted," Thane said in a shaky voice. "Just try not to channel Leighton anymore. You're terrifying."

Nikki gave him a weak grin and extended her left arm across the back of the seat until her fingertips brushed Corban's shoulder. *Sorry I went crazy. I didn't mean to take it out on Thane. Poor guy's already been through darkness.*

I don't blame you. I'm doing everything I can to hold it together. Corban focused on the road, driving as fast as he dared. They reached the edge of the lake and the main road south in minutes.

A flatbed truck filled with quarry stones was parked in front of the entrance to the bridge.

"We can move it—" Nikki started to say, but groaned when they drew close enough to see that all six tires were flat.

"Chaim isn't taking any chances," Thane said. "He doesn't want anyone to interfere with the launch."

Corban threw the truck into park and cut the engine. They climbed out and hesitated, staring down the length of the bridge, toward the landing strip.

"Listen," Nikki said. "Can you tell where they are?"

Thane shut his eyes in concentration. His face turned a shade paler than it already was. "I hear Solona."

TWENTY
COUNTDOWN

"What!" Nikki didn't wait for an explanation before she stuck her sword through a belt loop and ran to the front of the truck. She put one foot on the bumper and hoisted the other over the bridge railing.

"Wait!" Thane shouted, seizing the back of Corban's shirt before he could follow her. "Nikki, wait!"

She paused where she was, balanced on the railing, and gave him an incredulous look over her shoulder. "We can't wait! We have to get Mom away from the *Unity*!"

Thane took the apron away from his nose so they could both understand his words. "Once we start across the bridge, we *know* what's going to happen! We have to wait!"

"What will that accomplish?" Corban's brow was furrowed as he turned to Thane.

"For one thing, it'll give Solona time to get clear. She believes the premonition."

"What about Jing?" Nikki's voice was shrill. "If we wait, Kun'll have time to put her in a stasis pod!"

"The countdown's already started. I don't think he'll have time. Just give me a chance to listen." Thane didn't wait for them to respond before closing his eyes and focusing his Talent on the confrontation at the stairs to the *Unity*'s airlock. "Solona's arguing with Kun. She's telling him to give her Jing."

"You want your daughter to die with you?" Solona was pleading. "If you care so much about her, why would you risk killing her? You know the ship is going to blow up!"

"No one's going to die today," Kaczenski said. "The *Unity* is perfectly safe. Mechanics much wiser than you have been over every centimeter of it!"

"Corban saw—"

"Corban Abrams is a *liar!*" Kaczenski snapped. "All Strays are liars!"

"What if he's *right?*" Solona's tone turned cold. "You're willing to risk Jing's life to prove what? That you're an arrogant fool and a bigot who thinks more of his power and position than the lives of his own children?"

Ouch, Thane thought, *but someone needed to say it.*

"Please give me Jing. Leave if you're determined to go back to Earth, but give her a chance to live her own life. She has friends here; she's happy."

"She betrayed her father for those lying friends!" Kun said. "She belongs with her family!"

"What about Zhao?" Solona sounded furious. "Isn't he her family too? Isn't he your son? You think Jing will ever forgive you if she never sees him again?"

Kaczenski sputtered for a moment before a new voice joined in. "You're wasting your breath with her. She thinks all Strays are superhuman and deserve to be worshipped or something."

Thane opened his eyes and turned to Nikki. "Your father's joined the debate."

Nikki uttered a string of swear words, but Thane immediately switched his focus back to the confrontation outside the *Unity*.

"Get your brat inside the ship. We only have five minutes left to strap in before liftoff," Elian Ramirez said.

"Five minutes before you all die!" Solona hissed.

"You're delusional, but then you always have been. Get back if you think we'll blow, unless you'd like to go up in flames with us?" His laugh was scornful. "Move, Kun! We're on a tight schedule!"

"Please leave Jing!" Solona's voice cracked. "I'll look after her! I'll love her like my own daughter, I promise!"

"You could never love her like her own father." Kaczenski's reply was cold.

Thane heard the unmistakable sound of a pistol cocking. "Darkness! One of them has a gun!"

"I told you to get back!" Ramirez said. "Back away from the ship!"

A gunshot rang out, and Solona's scream filled the air, loud enough for Nikki and Corban to hear.

Nikki clamped a hand over her mouth. "Mom! Was she shot?"

Thane opened his eyes in time to see Nikki climb over the bridge railing to the other side of the truck. "We can't wait any longer!" she said.

"We have to!" Thane said. "She needs time to get away from the *Unity*!"

Corban climbed up on the truck bumper. "What do we do, Thane?"

"I need to listen." He squeezed his eyes shut. "Just one more minute."

214

The sounds of a struggle broke out, fists striking flesh, cries of pain and outrage. "What do you think you're doing?" Kaczenski asked. "She's *my* daughter! Let her go!"

Solona was gasping for breath, so Thane couldn't be sure if she'd been shot, but at least she wasn't dead. He heard a shocked grunt from Jing's father, followed by the sound of a body hitting the ground.

Was that Jing? Thane was numb with fear. He hated not being able to see what was happening.

The mechanical voice counting down announced, "Two minutes, fifteen seconds."

"You can both go to darkness! I'm sealing the ship!" Ramirez said.

Thane heard gears whining and the crisp metallic clang of the airlock being closed, followed by a string of profanities from Kaczenski. "I think Solona and Kun are still outside," he reported.

"Let's move!" Nikki said. "We can still save them!"

Corban clambered across the bridge railing to join her, a helpless, panicked look on his face. "We can't. Once we're standing on the bridge, it's over."

Thane bit his lip and rushed over to the truck. He propped his right knee on the bumper but couldn't swing his left leg over the railing. He slid across the hood on his stomach instead to reach the other side. Corban stepped over to catch him before Thane went facedown onto the bridge.

"Thanks." Thane got to his feet, looking down the long expanse of concrete to the Shrine. Fifty meters beyond it was the nose cone of the *Unity*.

"They've fired up the engines." He watched, paralyzed with fear, as the *Unity* began to shudder.

"This is insane." Tears rolled down Nikki's face. "We know how this ends." She gripped Corban's hand.

Without another word, they stood on the bridge together, Thane on Corban's left and Nikki on his right. "If Mom or Jing die because of Kun, I'll kill him myself—if he isn't dead already."

Thane had an absurd urge to laugh. He walked forward a few steps but stopped. Corban and Nikki also hesitated. They all knew it was dangerous to get too close.

"Should we wait?" Nikki's voice was heavy with uncertainty and fear. "Would it give them more time to escape?"

"The countdown's at fifteen seconds. I don't hear Solona or Kun." Thane was too afraid to listen for the AI to reach one. He made the decision to switch off his hearing just in time.

The force of the blast was more powerful than he imagined. Thane threw up his hands to shield his eyes even as he hit the bridge hard, thrown flat onto his back. A geyser of fire reached skyward before smoke engulfed the entire area, and obscured everything from view. He couldn't see the landing strip, the river, even the bridge. Hesitantly, he switched his hearing back on, only to be rewarded by Nikki's deafening scream.

"Nooooo!" She burst into tears, struggling to sit up. Her sword lay on the concrete a meter away from where she landed. She threw Thane a desperate look. "Mom? Jing?"

Corban managed to sit up, although he appeared dazed. He started to reach for Nikki but winced, groaned, and put a hand to the back of his head. His fingers came away covered in blood.

Thane searched for the apron to offer Corban, but he must have dropped it near the truck. He coughed as clouds of thick smoke drifted over them. He rolled onto his right side and pushed himself to an unsteady standing position.

"Can you hear anyone?" Nikki drew her knees up to her chin and lapsed into a fit of coughing. "Can you even hear me? My ears are ringing."

Thane brought the neck of his bloody T-shirt up over his mouth and nose. His eyes stung from the acrid smoke, but he had to close them anyway to focus his Talent.

What he heard was the crackling of a raging inferno, loud enough to drown out every sound for half a kilometer. Thane shook his head, realized Nikki couldn't see him through the haze, and tried to form an answer between coughs. "Nothing . . . we'll have to wait . . . until the smoke clears."

"What?"

He raised his voice and repeated the suggestion to wait.

Nikki sobbed harder. Corban managed to get his arms around her this time, and she buried her face in his shoulder. Thane moved closer and lowered himself onto his right knee. He put his arms around them, and they remained wrapped in a group hug for a few minutes, the dread of uncertainty washing over them like the suffocating blanket of smoke.

Thane was numb, unable to grieve without knowing for certain if Jing was dead. He had to cling to a sliver of hope, no matter how illogical or futile it seemed. The alternative was too horrible to imagine.

TWENTY-ONE
INFERNO

"We have to move closer." Nikki gently shrugged off two sets of arms and climbed to her feet. Her legs were trembling, but she wiped her eyes on her sleeve and forced herself to tap into whatever hidden reservoir of strength she could muster.

"What?" Corban squinted at her through the haze. "Closer? It's too dangerous."

"What?" Nikki hated the buzzing sound that filled her ears.

"I agree," Thane shouted, exchanging a determined frown with her. "Let's cover our faces and stay low."

Corban opened his mouth to object, but Nikki seized his hand so they could hear each other's thoughts. *Thane and I need to do this. We can't wait for the fire to go out. You understand?*

Of course I understand. Corban laced his fingers through hers. *But we'll need help.*

I'm sure help is coming. Nikki glanced toward the *Unity*, or what was left of it, which was still burning out of control, the flames reaching higher than the nose cone of the Shrine. *The whole colony must've heard the explosion.*

"You two need to let other people know what you're discussing!" Thane was uncharacteristically gruff. "Come on, we'll stay clear of the flames."

Nikki let go of Corban and hurried back to the truck. She climbed over the bridge railing and found the bloody yellow apron on the ground near the front bumper. "Toss me your shirts and I'll wet them in the river."

Thane and Corban exchanged raised eyebrows but quickly complied. Nikki slid down the weed-filled embankment, stooped down at the river's edge, dipped their T-shirts and her apron in the freezing water, wrung them out, and clambered back up to the bridge.

She climbed over the hood of the truck and handed their shirts back. "Let's do this." She wrapped the apron around her mouth and nose, using the ties to secure it at the back of her neck.

"I wish we had something to protect our eyes." Thane's nose had stopped bleeding, but it was difficult to tell from the blood-stained T-shirt covering his lower face. "Let's stay as low to the ground as possible." He led the way across the bridge.

Nikki took Corban's hand again, and they stayed close behind Thane.

The smoke was thicker the closer they got to the landing strip. Thane stooped down, and they imitated his stance. It was awkward, but it allowed them to catch an occasional breath of untainted air. When they reached the end of the bridge, they headed to the left, giving the *Unity* a wide berth.

Nikki kept her gaze on the abundant weeds growing through the cracks in the tarmac. Anytime she tried to straighten up, she was rewarded with stinging, watering eyes and a lungful of smoke. *I can't see a thing,* she told

Corban. *I'm scared we'll walk right by them. And it doesn't help that we can't hear.*

Thane can hear. Corban squeezed her hand.

Nikki tapped Thane's bare back and pointed to her ear when he turned to see what she wanted.

He nodded and paused, shutting his eyes. When he opened them again, he pointed off to the right and changed direction, leading the way.

Nikki squinted toward the *Unity* and bit her lip. All that was visible through the wall of smoke and flames was the steel framing, the girders glowing red from the heat. *Do you think the fire will spread to other ships?*

I don't know. The T-shirt over Corban's face muffled a rattling cough. *We can't stay out here much longer though.*

Without warning, Thane turned around and lunged at them, shoving them both to the tarmac. Corban let out a yelp as his bare back scraped the broken asphalt. A heartbeat later Nikki heard a thunderous rumbling, and the ground shook. A shower of sparks rained down on them from the collapsing ship.

Thane gasped as hot embers landed on his bare skin. Nikki shoved aside the arm pinning her and rolled out from beneath him. She whipped off the damp apron and used it to beat out the smoking cinders scattered across his back. Something hot landed on her scalp and another burned a hole through her T-shirt, singeing her left shoulder blade.

"We shouldn't be here!" Corban used his free hand to smother a spark on his own bare arm. "This is suicide!" He rolled to his feet and offered Thane a hand up.

Thane's eyes watered from the scorch marks blistering his back and shoulders, but he shook his head at Corban as soon as he was on his feet. He pointed the way they needed to go and started moving again, not waiting for a reply.

Nikki got the message and seized Corban's hand, pulling him along. She pressed the charred and blood-spattered apron back over her face, trying without success to draw in a lungful of breathable air. She knew Corban was right, but the thought of giving up before they found Solona and Jing wasn't an option.

"This way!" Thane reverted to his unusual skip-step maneuver to increase his speed without putting pressure on his left leg. Nikki and Corban gave up trying to keep their heads down and raced after him.

Nikki was relieved they were running away from the *Unity*'s inferno. Once they passed the library ship, the smoke thinned enough to see their destination: the hospital ship and—"*Mom! Jing!*"

Solona Zegarelli had reached the foot of the gang-way to the hospital ship, dragging an unconscious Jing on the tattered remains of her nurse's lab coat. She sank to the tarmac, sobbing, when she caught sight of Nikki.

Nikki put on a burst of speed and reached them first. "Mom!" She fell to her knees and threw her arms around her mother, who was covered with blisters and soot. "You're alive! What happened?" Solona's dark, chaotic, and terrifying memories of the past few minutes filled Nikki's mind, showing her everything before and after the *Unity* exploded. Nikki was slightly nauseated as she took it in, but she remained in awe of her mother's courage.

"Got to get . . . Jing inside," Solona managed between sobs.

For the first time Nikki noticed the bright red blood gushing from her mother's right thigh. "You're the one who needs to go inside! You've been shot!"

Thane reached Jing and scooped her up as if she weighed nothing, limping up the gangway without a pause. Corban helped Nikki pull Solona to her feet. They supported her between them, their wrists locked together behind her back.

Corban's eyes found Nikki's. *Where's Kun?*

Nikki shook her head, warning him not to say anything. She'd already seen the answer, but explanations would have to wait.

TWENTY-TWO
ASHES

Corban had been inside the hospital ship once in his life, to visit Thane when he was recovering from the loss of his left knee after the night terror attack. There was always a nurse on duty in the hospital. Today they were fortunate there was a doctor instead. "Dr. DeKalb!"

Lorna DeKalb materialized at the entryway the second the airlock cycled open. The tiny woman looked as if she'd been crying, but she assessed the motley group, with one sweep of her steel-gray eyes, and got right to work. "Solona!" She seized a gurney parked near the ladder and reached them in two strides. "Help me get her up," she ordered Nikki.

"What?" With a helpless expression, Nikki pointed to her ears.

DeKalb nodded, understanding. She raised her voice and repeated the request. She also took one look at Thane's burden and shouted, "Corban, grab the other gurney, near the lift!"

Corban hurried to do her bidding, heading down a short hallway where several wheelchairs and an extra gurney were pushed up against the wall.

"Put pressure on Solona's leg with this!" DeKalb handed him a bundle of gauze. "Hold it firmly, even if she squirms! Your head and back are bleeding. Sorry, but I'll have to take care of them later. Nikki, take her gurney to the lift, level three, get her into the surgical room, and get her prepped!"

DeKalb turned to his brother, who was leaning over Jing's gurney, holding her limp hand and looking helpless. "Put on your shirt, and where in darkness did you get all those burns?"

"The *Unity* exploded," Corban explained over his shoulder as he kept pace with Nikki's frenetic gurney driving. "You must've heard it," he called as they reached the lift.

He didn't hear DeKalb's reply as Nikki rushed them into the elevator and the doors snapped shut.

"Mom! Mom, can you hear me?"

Solona had lost consciousness somewhere between the airlock and the lift.

"She's lost a lot of blood!" Nikki put two fingers over the nurse's carotid artery. "Weak pulse. She dragged Jing all that way after my slime worm father shot her!"

"Do you know what happened to Kun?"

"Mom . . . tackled him *after* she'd been shot. She wrestled Jing away from him and left him on the ground. He didn't get clear of the ship." Nikki didn't elaborate. She got behind the gurney and moved fast once the lift doors parted. "We need to get Mom prepped for surgery!"

"We?" Corban felt a sudden chill, which wasn't because he'd just slipped his arms through the sleeves of his damp T-shirt.

"You wanted to learn more about the Medics Guild. Now's your chance."

A knot formed in his stomach. "Tell me what to do."

"Help me get her on the table, and grab those scissors so I can cut the jeans away from her wound."

Dr. DeKalb bustled into the room a few minutes later, tying a surgical gown at the back of her neck. She assessed their preparations, with a nod of approval, and continued to shout instructions. "Good job, Nikki!"

"Should I step out, ma'am?" Corban noticed DeKalb's stoic expression, her face almost as pale as the surgical mask she'd secured over her mouth and nose.

"No, I need your help! Find some gloves, and you can hand me instruments!" She uncovered the sterile tray Nikki wheeled to her side. "Nikki, I'll need you to be in charge of anesthesia! Tank is under there!" DeKalb waved a hand toward a lower bulkhead cabinet near the foot of the operating table.

"Her blood pressure is too low." Nikki tied a mask over her own face and tossed a second one to Corban.

"I'll have to numb the area and hope she doesn't wake up in the middle of surgery! There's no blood in storage!" DeKalb grimaced. "We'll have to pray she's strong enough to pull through."

Nikki extended her left arm, palm side up. "Mom and I share the same blood type. Please take some of mine."

The surgeon hesitated a heartbeat before snatching a syringe from the sterile tray. "Corban, move the gurney here, next to the table! Nikki, lie down!"

Corban did as DeKalb instructed for the next half hour, trying to keep his hands from shaking as he watched the blood flow from the IV in Nikki's arm to the one in Solona's. He averted his gaze as DeKalb pried the 9mm bullet from Solona's thigh. He handed her gauze and instruments, without looking too closely at the torn flesh and muscle fibers gaping from the hole in Solona's leg.

When DeKalb was stitching Solona's wound closed, Nikki broke the silence. "How's Jing?"

"I'm not sure what Kun used to sedate her, but she should be conscious soon," DeKalb said. "It's Thane I'm concerned about. I need to treat those burns and set his nose."

"Are you all right, ma'am?" Corban thought she looked ill.

"My husband . . . was on the *Unity*."

"I'm so sorry," Nikki said.

"That's why I'm here," the surgeon went on. "I told Jonah goodbye and wanted to watch the launch from a safe distance. The idiot was convinced the fuel rods were stable." Her eyes shifted to Corban's. "I told him several times about your premonition, and that the ship wasn't safe, but he fell for Chaim's lies. Jonah's always insisted our son's Talent was just his imagination, that no one can *smell* things from a distance like a night terror. He became obsessed with the idea of going back to Earth the instant Chaim mentioned it. He was even willing to leave me behind."

DeKalb studied the monitors on the wall measuring Solona's heart rate, respiration, and blood pressure. "Now nineteen people are dead." She paused, looking down at her unconscious colleague and friend. "Almost twenty."

"I'm sorry for your loss." Corban cleared his throat, trying to think of a tactful way to change the subject. "Should Nikki have some fluids?"

"Yes, there's a refrigerator over there." DeKalb blinked away a few tears and waved her free hand in the direction of a bulkhead cabinet. "She'll need juice; orange, if there's any."

"Can I sit up?" Nikki asked.

"No!" Corban and DeKalb said in the same breath. "You just gave your mother a liter of blood," the doctor added. "You'll lie there until I see some color in your cheeks."

"Yes, ma'am." Nikki's eyes found Corban's. She extended her untethered arm toward him.

He sandwiched her cold fingers between his palms. *You were very brave to offer your own blood.*

She studied her mother's ashen face. *I just hope it was enough.*

Corban managed to get half a liter of orange juice into Nikki before she fell into an exhausted slumber. Dr. DeKalb applied a painkiller patch to Solona's leg and then took a minute to bandage his head wound and the cuts on his back before leaving him in the surgical room with the women. She left strict instruction to call her on the ship's intercom if Solona's blood pressure or heart rate dropped.

"I don't want to move her until she's more stable. I'm going to check on Jing and treat your brother's burns. Solona's going to hurt like darkness when she wakes up, so notify me the moment she does."

"Yes, ma'am." Corban found a folding chair and sat where he could observe all of Solona's monitors and still reach Nikki's hand. Her mind was quiet while she slept, so he took a few minutes to do a self-assessment.

It hurt to breathe. His lungs were congested, as if he had bronchitis or pneumonia, and his eyes were gritty and irritated from the smoke. He was sure they were as bloodshot as Nikki's had been before she dozed off. The burn on his forearm throbbed, but he knew Thane hurt more with his multiple burns and broken nose. Corban was exhausted, but grateful the people he cared about had survived the *Unity*'s explosion. He wondered how Zhao and Jing would take the news that their father didn't survive. Jing, no doubt, would produce enough waterworks to power a fort. Nikki's father was dead too, but he suspected that wouldn't phase her.

Good thing the trashbird was a lousy shot. He thought of his own brush with death at Ramirez's hands. Solona's wound was serious, but he suspected a few physical therapy sessions with Nehal Hong would have her up and walking soon enough. He was grateful the PT was able to convince her husband not to go on the *Unity*. Vesta couldn't afford to lose any medics. *Especially not now, with this infertility issue.*

Infertility. He mulled the word over in his mind, and his imagination wandered. He released Nikki's hand, just to be certain she couldn't hear his thoughts. There would be a time to tell her about his latest premonition, *maybe when we're older.*

Much older.

***

A door to the left of the surgical suite opened to a post-op room furnished with a hospital bed and some equipment for an IV and the like, but Corban walked straight past it to the tiny port window in the bulkhead wall. He had to squint to see out. It was getting dark, and smoke still hung over the entire landing strip, drifting and swirling in patches that were sometimes thick, obstructing his view.

He stared at the area beyond the library ship until the breeze thinned the smoke enough for him to see the smoldering pile of wreckage that used to be the

Unity. Bent and blackened steel beams and huge piles of ash were all that was left of the ship.

A dozen people in firefighting gear combed the edges of the embers. The colony's only fire truck was parked nearby, the long hose snaking out of sight toward the river, although it was obvious to Corban that any efforts to contain the blaze were too little, too late.

He spotted something on the tarmac between the *Unity*'s ashes and the library gangway. A familiar lone figure stood sentinel beside a blue tarp draped over a man-sized lump.

"Thane," Corban whispered, knowing his brother could hear him without the intercom, "you need to go outside and tell Zhao his sister's safe. I guess when she wakes up, you'll need to tell her . . ."

Thane's bleak reply came over the speaker in the ceiling. "Tell her she's an orphan now, just like us."

TWENTY-THREE
RESPITE

Thane and Zhao sat on opposite edges of the hospital bed, surreptitiously avoiding each other's eyes. Thane massaged Jing's feet through the blanket, but Zhao kept throwing him disapproving looks every few minutes.

"What?" Thane lost patience. "It's just her feet." He hated that he sounded as if he had a bad head cold, but with the congestion from the smoke inhalation and both nostrils packed with gauze, it couldn't be helped.

"This is ridiculous." Jing was sitting up in the bed, pillows propped behind her, arms folded across her chest. "You two don't have to hover over me all night. I'm fine."

"Dr. DeKalb told us to keep an eye on you, *mei mei*," Zhao said.

"It's a little late for that!" she snapped. "Solona was the one who rescued me."

"Sorry," both young men muttered, avoiding each other's gaze.

"I should've gotten there faster," Thane said. "I could've stopped him."

"I should've known *Baba* was up to something and kept you from meeting him," Zhao added before Jing could reply.

Jing blinked back tears for the first time since hearing the news of Kun's death an hour ago. Thane had been expecting this, but he felt like a third wheel. He knew the siblings needed each other during this time of grief. He slowly got to his feet and turned toward the door.

"No, don't go." Jing held out a hand to him. "Please stay."

Thane turned to Zhao for advice, but his friend wouldn't meet his eyes. Zhao dipped his chin, indicating resignation more than acquiescence, but Thane experienced a flutter of relief. He wanted Zhao's approval, even though Jing's brother insisted her personal life wasn't any of his business.

He moved to Jing's side and took her outstretched hand in both of his, wincing a bit from a slight pressure on a burn at the base of his left thumb.

Jing murmured, "Sorry." She attempted to pull him into a full embrace, but there were too many burns on his back.

"Sorry." Thane stifled a gasp as he wriggled free of her arms. "I'll just hold your hand."

His pain appeared to halt her tears, and she studied his face with a concerned frown. "Can you hold me?" She scooted over as far as she could on the narrow bed, creating a decimeter of space for him.

Thane made a point of not looking at Zhao as he squeezed in beside her and put both arms around her, taking care not to lean back against the pillows. It was awkward, but it seemed to please her. She pressed the side of her face against his chest and sniffled a few times but, surprisingly, didn't cry.

After a long silence, Zhao cleared his throat. "I'm going to find a place to sleep. Nikki told me there're dozens of empty beds in the hospital."

"Goodnight, *ge'-ge'*. I love you."

"Love you too, *mei mei*." Zhao slipped out of the room.

Thane was tempted to echo the phrase, but this wasn't the time or place. There was too much physical and emotional pain to cope with. He couldn't even kiss her because he couldn't breathe through his nose, and with his twin black eyes and face still streaked with soot, he was amazed she could bear to look at him.

Solona's conscious, Rupert's voice interrupted his thoughts. *Doc thinks she's going to be all right. Corban and I are heading upstairs to find places to sleep. See you in the morning.*

We all made it through another one of Corban's nightmares. Thane's gratitude was overshadowed by exhaustion. He couldn't keep his eyes open. "I'll see you in the morning." He eased himself out of the narrow bed, doing his best to ignore Jing's disappointed pout. "Goodnight."

"I want to see you every morning," Jing's tone turned sultry, "for the rest of our lives."

Thane managed a timid, "Maybe," as he slipped from the room.

Maybe? He shook his head as he climbed the central ladder to a higher level that was quiet and presumably unoccupied. *Could I be any more pathetic?* He tried a door just off the ladder and found a tiny room with a bed. As he took off his brace and boots and stretched out on his stomach, he focused his Talent out of habit, assessing the aftermath of the tragedy.

Night terrors growled outside the ship despite the heat from the *Unity*'s dying embers. Thane opened his eyes in the darkness, his heart pounding again.

ACKNOWLEDGEMENTS

Thank you to my family for giving me the time and quiet I need to write. Thanks to my beta readers, authors Lisa Rector, Tamara Ward, and Jandy Salguero. I appreciate the hard work of my cover artist, Jessica Phillips, who can turn Rylee Jensen's photos and my crazy concepts into a work of art. Thanks again to my cover models, Jared Weaver, Aaron Weaver, and Jayden Beach, and to my map artist, author Cindy Clark. My biggest thanks go to my talented cousin, author Lisa Rector, who also worked hard as my editor and formatter. I've come to rely so much on her advice and keen eye that I honestly couldn't get my books into print without her help.

SterlingRWalker.com

www.ingramcontent.com/pod-product-compliance
Lightning Source LLC
Chambersburg PA
CBHW072351190626
46811CB00019B/492